Gardens

Ian Nicholson

ISBN: 978-0-244-51389-4

PublishNation
www.publishnation.co.uk

Cover illustration: **Ian Nicholson**

www.moderngothicwriter.com

This book is dedicated to the memory of Mike Kennerley, a dear friend and a keen gardener.

INDEX

THE PROCESS

'I can honestly say that I've never seen such magnificent gladioli, Alison. Don't you agree, darling?'

Roger grudgingly accepted that his wife was right but could only manage a thin smile and a brief nod by way of response. Marion's next comment made him grind his teeth with annoyance.

'Why, they're even bigger than your prize-winners at the County Show last year, and everyone thought *they* were impressive!'

Roger instantly lost himself in the memory of that happy weekend. He basked in the satisfying glow of a personal victory when all competition had simply melted away, and he recalled the moment when he first noticed the gilt-edged card next to his display. Forced back into the present by an insistent nudge from Marion, Roger felt under pressure to speak to the newest resident on Tenison Road.

'Well the judge did tell me that they were the best blooms he'd encountered for many a year which, I suppose, does set me apart from most growers in the county....'

The arrogant little man paused to let his statement achieve full impact, but Alison didn't respond as he had hoped. In fact, she hardly seemed to be listening at all, focusing instead on the far end of the garden in a kind of trance. Roger loudly cleared his throat, determined to make this woman pay attention. Alison slowly turned her eyes towards him, and he continued.

'I suppose your efforts are worthy of *some* appreciation, but then size isn't everything is it, Alison?'

If he hadn't been so wrapped up in his own importance, Roger might have noticed a sarcastic smile flickering across Marion's face. He offered a half compliment.

'I have to admit that yours *are* larger than mine, but I find the colours a little gaudy for my taste.'

'Oh, come on, darling! Some of yours virtually looked the same, only just a little smaller!'

Roger winced. He had always disliked it when Marion used terms of endearment in public, but her comment about the size of his prize-winning flowers added feelings of inadequacy to his embarrassment. He privately wished his wife would stop talking but she carried on, seemingly enjoying his discomfort.

'Besides, if anything Alison has achieved a much wider colour palette than you did over several years, and this is her first full summer! I'd love to take a little walk around your garden, dear. Would that be alright?'

'Yes of course, Mrs. Crawford. I'll come with you. How about your husband? He's looking rather flushed.'

'Oh, call us Roger and Marion, please, and don't worry about *him*. He never could stand coming second best in anything. Are you staying here, darling?'

Maybe it was the August sun beating down relentlessly on his balding pate (he had ignored Marion's advice to bring his sun hat and to fetch it now would amount to a defeat), or maybe it was the almost intoxicating mix of warm, wafting scents that assailed his nostrils. Whatever the reason, Roger found himself hot and bothered in the extreme, unable to respond to his wife's question. Instead he remained seated on the dark green, wrought iron bench, and watched as the two women set off across the perfectly mown lawn.

Roger poured himself a glass of home-made lemonade and placed the jug back on the table. He distractedly stared at the diminishing ice cubes as they jiggled in his tumbler and thought back to last year when this patch of land was in a sorry state indeed.

A broken-down lawnmower in the far corner, shattered glass from a long-abandoned greenhouse and weeds holding sway over the whole area. All the other gardens in Tenison Road were tended beautifully and developed with love and care, over decades in some cases. Only No. 37 had been left to fend for itself with no green-fingered attention lavished on it for years, although older residents wistfully remembered a time when things were very different.

Jean Baker had inherited the house from her father. Fred had always enjoyed his garden and was almost self-sufficient thanks to the abundant produce he grew there, so when he passed away his daughter vowed to maintain his horticultural standards. As he had done, Jean took pleasure in distributing the fruits of her labour amongst the residents of Tenison Road, a gesture that was always appreciated. When old age eventually set in, however, working in the garden became more of a burden than a pleasure and it soon started to fall into disrepair. Her son Michael lived only half an hour's drive away and used to help his mother whenever he could, but he moved out of the area due to starting a new job in London. Jean died three years later, and by then the garden had fallen into a pronounced state of decay.

When the 'For Sale' board went up, neighbours hoped that whoever took over the property would keep the weeds down at the very least, agreeing that it would be even better if a keen gardener moved into No. 37. Several potential buyers came to view the house, but it was over six months before Alison first expressed an interest. During this period of uncertainty, Marion became increasingly irritated by a new behaviour from her husband (one to add to her list of many that surfaced throughout their 42 years of reasonably happy marriage). As they prepared for bed, Roger would draw back the left-hand curtain along with the nets, look down on the row of gardens and sigh heavily. Marion was fully aware that a response from her was expected, and knew that the conversation would always run along familiar, rather tedious lines:

'What's wrong, dear?'

'It's just that…. Oh, I wish someone would hurry up and buy that damned place and tidy up the mess down there! I mean it's not asking much is it, Marion? Tenison Road is such a quiet place and we all get on with each other around here, so I felt *sure* that it would have been sold by now. Do you know what that so-called garden reminds me of, Marion?'

Every time Roger asked her this question, she wanted to scream back:

'YES OF COURSE I DO, BECAUSE YOU ASK ME AT LEAST TWICE EVERY BLOODY WEEK! NOW CLOSE THE CURTAIN AND COME TO BED BEFORE I THROW SOMETHING AT YOU!'

Instead she would quietly answer:

'What does it remind you of, Roger?'

'A perfect row of teeth, apart from one that's been allowed to rot and turn black! *That's* what I see down there, Marion!'

Even though she found these discussions particularly annoying, she had to admit that it wasn't a bad analogy. Sometimes, just before Marion closed the bedroom curtains in the late evening, she would look along the perfectly tended plots below and stare at the solid tangle of weeds at No. 37. Not much light fell upon the gardens as night descended, so the overgrown area indeed appeared almost black in comparison with the others. Marion, usually a calming influence in the home, found herself becoming as tense as her husband over the property issue. It wasn't that she was overly bothered about how long the house sale was taking. No, her frustration grew each time she had to watch her husband standing at the window, pointlessly getting angry over something that would eventually be resolved and was out of his control anyway.

All on the odd-numbered side of Tenison Road were delighted when the 'Sold' sign was erected, but especially the couple at No. 31, Roger because something might finally be done about the 'bloody jungle', and Marion because she wouldn't have to listen to his bedtime rants anymore. Everyone found Alison to be charming and welcomed her warmly, not least because she had started to clear the weeds within the first week of moving into No. 37. This was particularly satisfying to Roger who felt the natural order of things had been restored, something he raised over breakfast one morning.

'It's wonderful that Alison's – well – one of us, isn't it, Marion?'

'Whatever do you mean?'

'A fellow horticulturalist! Someone who appreciates and understands the importance of a well-maintained garden! I mean, we could have ended up with a neighbour who just left the space as it was. Think about that!'

Marion spread butter and marmalade over a burnt piece of toast and savoured the scents of citrus and charcoal before answering.

'I *do* see what you mean, Roger, but would it really have mattered so much?'

'It might not matter to you, but the look of the neighbourhood and especially the gardens is why I've always enjoyed living here. I thought you felt the same, Marion.'

She slowly sipped the last of her coffee and looked at the man sitting opposite. For more than a year now, Marion had found it increasingly hard to engage with Roger on any level. Conversations were often stale and repetitive, and she felt that her life had become veneered with a grey blandness. Sometimes she would sit in the conservatory and think back to a happier time, a time when she would encourage Roger to compete in flower shows around the county. Marion always accompanied him to these events, sharing in his frequent success in achieving gold status and consoling him on the rare occasions when he failed ('Come on, darling, even a bronze isn't *bad*....'). She hadn't even attended the last three competitions, feigning migraines and relieved to have some peace and quiet. Now, on this morning like any other, she couldn't even be bothered to reply. Instead she stood to clear the breakfast table with a shrug.

To Marion's disappointment, Roger's night-time inspection of the dishevelled garden was simply replaced with a daily commentary on Alison's progress. She would find him upstairs, staring from his vantage point behind the net curtains at their neighbour as she worked outside. If anything, this was even worse than his previous activity, because Roger insisted on giving his wife an almost running commentary on No. 37's 'redevelopment' at mealtimes. Marion gradually trained herself to filter out these details and focus on her food, but something made her pay attention when he spoke about what lay at the end of Alison's garden one morning after breakfast.

'You know it's strange, Marion. She's been digging in loads of compost whenever she plants anything, but the size of the heap seems to stay the same. Well, to be precise, when I look out every morning it has returned to its original proportions. Sometimes I could swear its even grown a little larger. Curious, don't you think?'

'What *I* think is you're spending far too much time concerning yourself with someone else's business! Now help me load the dishwasher!'

She flashed a look of contempt at Roger and silence fell between them, but Marion's curiosity had certainly been sparked. It didn't make sense. How could a pile of decomposing material replenish itself overnight?

It wasn't long before Alison's garden became the envy of her immediate neighbours and the topic of conversation for everyone on Tenison Road. No-one could explain how her plants

6

had not only established themselves so quickly, but also the vibrancy and rapidity of her blooms. Green-fingered Roger still looked down from the bedroom window each day, but now the green-eyed monster stood at his shoulder, whispering its poisonous, jealousy-laden questions in his ear. How did Alison manage to create such incredible results over such a short space of time? What had she got that he hadn't, and why didn't anyone come to marvel at *his* garden anymore?

For fellow gardeners often used to call in at No. 31 just to view Roger's impressive floral achievements. How he revelled in their appreciative comments, affecting modesty but all the while feeling 'best of the bunch' himself, an attitude Marion had found completely nauseating for months. Recently all that adulation, along with every expression of delight and surprise, had fallen like the petals from a prize-winning rose after a competition. Roger just wasn't used to this sensation of fading away and he didn't like it one bit, which is why he agreed to accompany his wife on a visit to No. 37.

Marion had met Alison in the local bakery two days ago, and the invitation had been offered and accepted during their conversation. Roger refused to attend when the arrangement was first mentioned, only to be immediately chastised by Marion.

'You're coming and that's an end to it! I know – oh, do I *know* – how annoyed you are that Alison's garden is the talk of the road, but that's no reason to sulk like a little schoolboy. I suggest, my darling, that you practice putting on a warm, neighbourly smile because you're going to need it!'

Since then, however, Roger realised that this occasion afforded him a rare opportunity. At last he could investigate the roots of his neighbour's gardening success. He might even be able to use any secrets uncovered there himself, thus re-establishing Roger Crawford as the definitive Gold Standard of Tenison Road. That dream tasted *so* good and he found himself counting down the hours to 'Project Unearth', a title of which he was secretly proud but one he would never reveal to Marion.

Now, as Roger watched Alison guide his delighted wife around the garden, he thought he saw a slight disturbance near the back fence. His eyes had been drawn there after hearing a single shriek from some animal, which he assumed to be a cat. This was confirmed with a sudden flash of a striped tail but nothing more. He turned his attention to the two women who were laughing and discussing various plants along the path. They were clearly getting along famously and hadn't noticed the sound or sight at all. Slightly unnerved, Roger decided to join Alison and her guest as they stopped near an impressive display of hollyhocks and delphiniums, their height imposing and dramatic.

'Ah, here you are! These are amazing, aren't they, Roger? Just look at these brilliant blue ones, and the purples over there! Are you listening, Roger?'

He ignored his wife's questions, troubled by something seen out of the corner of his eye. Roger was sure of more movement in the same place as before, although this appeared to be a succession of slight tremors near the ground. He tried to convince himself that it was only heat haze but didn't fully succeed. Instead he turned to his hostess with a question he had been aching to ask.

'Tell me, Alison, how have you managed to grow these wonderful displays in such a short space of time? You've clearly entranced Marion here as well as most of Tenison Road, so I'm forced to wonder if your secret is wrapped up in magic – black, white or green!'

Alison ignored the sarcasm-laced politeness of his enquiry and offered the simplest of explanations.

'There's no magic involved, Mr. Crawford. Just honest toil and a joy in the process of gardening.'

Roger rankled slightly at the formal use of his name and felt that his question had been somehow dismissed as ridiculous. He considered her phrase 'the process of gardening' to be rather odd but decided to press her further.

'Come on, Alison! There must be more to it than that! I insist you tell me!'

'Roger! That's ENOUGH! You just can't accept that someone could possibly be better at gardening than you, can you? I'm sorry for my husband's behaviour, Alison. *I've* really enjoyed this afternoon so thank you for showing me round. Come on, you – we're going home!'

Marion grabbed Roger's arm and all but dragged him down the garden. The intense colours merged into one blurry rainbow in his eyes and he temporarily couldn't remember where he was. His wife forced him through the side garden gate, and Alison listened as Marion started screaming abuse as they walked away. She turned to cast a glance towards the end of her garden and smiled.

'Project Unearth' hadn't been a failure, Roger told himself the following morning as he relaxed with Marion on the patio. It just needed a new approach, that's all. The more he thought about it the more he wanted to know Alison's gardening secrets.

'It's no good, Marion. I must find out how she does it!'

Marion ignored him. She turned the page of her Sunday supplement and considered the recipe for Beef Wellington displayed on page 17, but decided it looked too complicated to prepare. If this scene were in a cartoon, Roger would have had steam coming out of his ears.

'MARION!'

'I heard you, Roger, but after your little performance at Alison's I'm simply not interested in anything you do or say, and I *certainly* don't want to know about any little schemes you're hatching in that tiny brain of yours.'

9

'Fine! FINE!'

With that, Roger threw down his newspaper and went indoors to cool his temper, leaving Marion quietly giggling to herself.

In the afternoon, with the dishwasher rumbling away in the kitchen, Marion went back outside to enjoy the sunshine. The meal, for the most part, had been conducted in silence and both parties were glad when it ended. Roger went through to the study and poured a large brandy. He sank down into a black leather armchair and savoured the rich oak aromas rising from the glass before emptying it in one. The liquid burned his throat, but he didn't mind, for it was at this point that 'Project Unearth' snapped into focus.

'OF COURSE!'

Roger put the glass on the floor, leapt up from his chair and clapped his hands together like a child.

The reason for Alison's achievements had to be the seemingly unremarkable pile of decomposing material sitting near her back fence. Roger already thought it odd how the compost heap changed back to its original proportions after use, but now he considered its colour. Compared to his own, No. 37's appeared positively black, almost sinister now he came to think about it.

He sifted through the memories of yesterday's visit and tried to remember the decomposing shape's texture, but this proved impossible as there had been no surface details on which to focus. In hindsight, it seemed to Roger that the heap was no more than a void or something akin to a black hole, a disturbing thought indeed. Nevertheless, he knew that he just had to investigate further in order to satisfy his curiosity.

'The sooner the better, Roger. It's the only way.'

He smiled as he poured another drink, relieved that Marion hadn't heard him talking to himself. His expression changed to one of seriousness, however, when the next thought took hold.

'Marion must never, *never* know about this, that's for sure.'

With a plan already forming in his mind, Roger emptied his glass (in two this time) and left the study, whistling as he closed the door.

The evening passed pleasantly enough. They watched a reasonably good detective thriller on BBC1, spoilt by Marion's somewhat inane questions about the plot's machinations:

'Wasn't Stephanie out shopping in the village when Julian got shot?'

'Why was that Mr. Frobisher out until past midnight?'

'Where did Susan's twin sister Sarah rush off to in such a hurry after the barbecue?'

Oh, why couldn't the woman keep up? The story wasn't that complicated, Roger thought. He had worked out long before the denouement that Anita Hedges was the killer, using the revolver that belonged to her lover Colonel Roberts. As the credits rolled, Marion went through to the kitchen to make mugs of hot chocolate, leaving Roger to run through his little scheme once more.

The digital bedroom clock displayed 02:48 as Roger slowly crept out of bed, determined not to disturb Marion. He had managed to sleep only lightly, so keen was he to undertake 'Project Unearth Mk2'. He stepped into his slippers, grabbed his dressing gown and keys and tiptoed downstairs.

Roger took a spoon and a small, screw top jar from the kitchen and left the house, pulling the front door to as quietly as possible.

He was delighted to find that the side gate at No. 37 had no lock, so he gingerly lifted the latch and entered the garden.

The heady perfume of night-scented stock, redolent of talcum powder and great aunts' bedrooms, hung in the air to greet him. As he walked silently over the lawn, Roger observed the floral display on either side. Each bloom was partially shadowed in the moonlight and appeared even larger than before. This rather unnerved the intruder, but he strode forward with renewed purpose.

Roger stood before Alison's compost heap and was struck by the range of smells that instantly assailed his nostrils. He leaned forward and sniffed deeply, trying to ascertain the individual elements as he raised his head. Coffee? Tar? Burnt toast? His own compost at No. 31 hardly smelt of anything, and he'd read somewhere that action was required if a heap smelt of ammonia, but this was extraordinary.

Two cats yowled and hissed at each other a few fences down which snapped Roger out of his olfactory musings. He nervously looked up at several windows to see if the noisy felines had disturbed anyone's sleep, but neither lights came on nor curtains twitched. Back to his mission, then.

Roger unscrewed the silver lid from the jar and paused for a moment. At last he had a chance to work out just what was in this wonder material. He'd always fancied himself as a bit of a detective, solving much more complicated cases than those written for television (and far beyond Marion's attempts at deduction). Apart from anything else, his horticultural pride was at stake here and he was determined to become 'top of the heap' again.

This thought amused Roger and he allowed himself a low chuckle as he moved the spoon towards the compost. Within a few seconds he had disappeared, a startled cry briefly breaking the silence. After that, all that remained of 'Project Unearth Mk2' was a tartan slipper, dislodged during the attack.

She presses her black shiny nose against the base of the dark loamy material in search of food and listens to her two cubs chasing each other on the moonlit lawn. She investigates a partly decomposed apple and savours the heady scent of fermentation, unaware of two gnarled tendrils silently emerging nearby. The first wraps itself around her back legs whilst the other reaches up and twists around her bushy orange, white-tipped tail. Within moments she is gone. Her cubs stop their play and move towards the end of the garden in search of her, whimpered calls echoing in the night air. They reach the end of the garden and one becomes briefly distracted by a highly patterned slip-on shoe.

A HEALTHIER OPTION

At last a chance! She could hardly contain her excitement at the prospect of eating again. They were twins and 12 years old or thereabouts, but she could see that the boy already had some meat on his bones. The old woman licked her dry lips, peered through the translucent yellow and red windowpanes and concentrated on willing the pair to step inside the garden.

She could see that they were impressed. Why wouldn't they be? The gingerbread structure took a long time to finish, the filigree work in white icing alone taking over a fortnight. Already in her mid-nineties and fading fast, she had mustered most of what little magic remained in her to create the walls. Her powers were further diminished as intense hunger grew, so she had been forced to cook, cut and shape the latter parts of her project by hand. Brownies, biscuits, cakes – *everything* proved to be an exhausting struggle, and at times she wondered if it was all worthwhile.

Eventually, even lifting the heavy trays from the large oven became a problem. She tried to ignore both her weakness and her rumbling stomach whilst working, but the restless nights were even worse. Tempting visions of steaming roasts assailed her dreams and she would wake with a start on each occasion, aching for them to be real but forced to acknowledge her pain instead.

On the day the house was completed, over three months ago, the old crone flopped down into a soft marshmallow armchair and hoped that her luck would change soon.

Well now, it seemed, it had.

She watched as the boy moved closer to the heavy chocolate door, decorated with sugar-spun roses and realistic woodgrain effect (she had been particularly bored one Monday afternoon). A long drool of saliva left her mouth and landed on the coconut ice floor tiles. She could almost taste him. He tentatively reached towards the candy twist bell-pull when the girl called out to him from the garden.

'Hey! Look at these!'

He turned to see, withdrew his hand and walked towards his sister to investigate further. The aged sorceress was so angry that she knocked a white chocolate vase off the biscuit table. It shattered on impact and she was temporarily distracted by the pale shards at her feet, but the intense need for meat drew her gaze back to the window.

It appeared that they were eating something, as far as she could tell. The wizened hag moved to the front door and lifted the peanut brittle letterbox in order to listen to their conversation. The girl spoke first.

'This one tastes of honey and it's really good. Try one!'

'I'm not sure we should *eat* anything. I mean, this isn't our garden and....'

'You drive me crazy sometimes! Listen to me. Mother's always telling us to eat more healthily which is exactly what we're doing here. Besides we're doing the owner a favour by keeping the weeds down, right?'

The boy nodded as his sister snapped off another flapjack and passed it to him. He hesitantly took a bite, intrigued not only to find oats but also a variety of seeds contained in the mixture. Within moments he had devoured the rest of it and reached for another.

Tired eyes watched as the children giggled and ate more of the garden's healthy snacks spread before them. Soon they had stripped the flapjack plants bare so started to feast on the abundant rice cakes growing nearby instead. The old biddy's rage intensified, heightened by frustration and puzzlement. Why had these plants grown in her garden? Was it due to a spell malfunction or had the house itself turned against its creator?

This last thought made a modicum of sense to her. The building had not been a labour of love in any sense, love not even being in a witch's vocabulary, but one of pure necessity. Resentment had gradually grown within the walls as to how long everything was taking, and she often felt that the very structure was mocking her rapidly failing powers. As she watched the children feasting, she realised that the weeds were a result of magic harnessed by the property and redirected against her. The bony bewitcher wasn't exactly sure how this had happened, but she *was* sure of one thing. Any chance of a piping hot meal was fading fast and she knew drastic action was required.

She let go of the letterbox and slowly opened the door, forcing a smile and displaying her four remaining teeth. The boy saw the old woman first and nudged his sister. They both looked at her as she moved towards them, primarily focusing her attentions on the young male.

'What's your name, dearie?'

'I'm....'

'Don't tell her! She looks like pure evil to me and you know we mustn't talk to strangers.'

The witch's smile evaporated, and she turned her cold hungry eyes towards the girl.

'You're both trespassing on private property so watch your tongue, young lady!'

She paused for a moment, savouring the thought of eating their succulent, taste bud-laden organs, possibly as a starter. The near toothless grin returned, and the stooped old crow employed a softer tone of voice.

'I'll tell you what. Just step inside and we'll say no more about it. You don't really want to eat this healthy rubbish, do you? Especially when I've got so many treats in there just waiting to be enjoyed....'

She waited for a response and could see that the boy was tempted. Almost crazed with hunger, she eagerly watched him take two steps towards the house, but her dream of a lengthy spell in the kitchen was dashed by his sister.

'You must think we're totally stupid! We live on the edge of these woods, and we've heard stories about people like you from our parents. Come on, brother, let's find our way home. I know we don't always get on, but your idea of marking every third tree with your penknife was a really good one!'

The siblings smiled sweetly at each other which made the old harpy feel rather nauseous. She moved towards the open front door, cursing wildly as she did so. She stepped inside and heard the boy thank her for the snacks before the pair left the denuded garden, hand in hand.

She slammed the door so hard that three of the sugar roses fell off and several chocolate brownie roof tiles crashed to the ground. Much more disconcerting was the way the gingerbread walls trembled with cruel laughter at her failure. She knew that it could be weeks or even months before fresh meat happened to pass by, especially as those two brats would tell everyone about their experience.

The enchantress wearily looked around her front room at the gaudy trappings and furnishings, all fashioned from sugary temptation. She flopped down into the mallow armchair, hungry beyond reason and utterly deflated. That hearty meal, she felt sure, would have restored her powers of magic, resulting in positive change throughout. Everything appeared within her grasp when the children arrived, but the garden weeds had defeated her in ways she could not have imagined. Damn fat-free and healthy options!

There was nothing else for it. She weakly rolled up the left sleeve of her ragged black dress and sank her heavily stained teeth into wrinkled flesh. A few red drops splashed onto the pink and white flooring. Desperate times, they always say, call for desperate measures.

MOMENTS

Fiona let out a cry of delight in the hallway when she read the letter. She had applied for an allotment almost a year ago and had all but given up hope of receiving one, so this was welcome news indeed. When she considered buying the flat, the lack of a garden was the only negative she could see. The location was perfect, being just six tube stops away from work and reasonably close to sister Maddy, two years her junior.

Fiona initially found London to be a cold and lonely place where hardly anyone went out of their way to offer a smile, let alone friendship. She had moved there from Edinburgh two years ago aged 33, having secured an editing role at a large publishing house. She was used to the work, which was rewarding and fully engaged her, but it was during the lonely evenings that doubts about her relocation crept into Fiona's thoughts. Coupled with these was the longing for familiar landscapes and landmarks. She particularly missed the castle atop its great rock and dominating the city skyline, but also simple pleasures like window shopping on Princes Street. Sometimes the ache for home became so intense that she would look up train times on her laptop, until dreams of stepping onto the platform at Edinburgh Waverley chased her isolation away, momentarily at least.

Fiona's life greatly improved when Maddy moved to London. Their parents had passed away four years before within a few weeks of each other, and the sisters had remained close ever since. Maddy had often cried down the phone to her London-based sibling, explaining through her tears how much she missed her and the bond between them. After several such emotional phone calls, Fiona decided to offer Maddy a room in her flat which had, for the most part, been bought using Fiona's inheritance.

It soon became clear that this was the right decision. In fact, the pair got on better than ever, reminiscing about childhood and schooldays as well as exploring London together. They often cooked Scottish food or gave English meals a Caledonian twist, adding whisky to gravies or mixing broken shortbread into crumble toppings. The sisters enjoyed developing new recipes and the results usually tasted great, but after each meal a wistful silence would spread between them. Neither woman needed to speak or ask what the other was thinking. Homesick blues had taken a seat at their kitchen table, as ever the uninvited guest.

Maddy had a bright, open personality and found a job as a bar manager in Covent Garden. She thrived in the role, having worked in similar employment in Edinburgh. Fiona would often drop by after leaving the office and was always impressed by how Maddy engaged so effortlessly with the customers, but what she didn't know was just *how* much her sister had been engaging with one of them.

After seeing her disarming smile for the first time, Gavin knew that he just had to ask Maddy out for dinner. By the fifth date, he had asked her to move in with him and she had joyfully accepted. He worked in finance and had a large flat in North London with plenty of room to spare. A quick mover, one could say, but they both felt the same about each other and were excited about their new living arrangements. All that remained for Maddy was to tell Fiona the news. Although happy for them both (she had met Gavin and really liked him), Fiona knew that it was back to square one as far as her social life was concerned. Yes, she got on well with her colleagues and occasionally went out with them, but none made her feel *alive* like Maddy did. Oh, and how she would miss their Scottish culinary adventures, laughing and being creative in the kitchen together.

After only six months of her sister's leaving, Fiona decided to sell the flat and move closer to Maddy and Gavin. She was always made to feel welcome when visiting the couple but missed Maddy's presence even more as soon as she arrived home.

The search for a new place to live brought with it the possibility of owning a garden, however small. One of the memories she held close in her heart was that of her parents' large garden, and the pride they took in its upkeep and development over many years. Fiona viewed several properties before deciding to go for another flat, and although disappointed that her second purchase didn't even have a communal green space, she was more than intrigued when a colleague first mentioned allotment gardening, hence her excitement over this letter from the council.

Fiona could hardly wait to get started. Within a week of receiving her confirmation, she had visited the site and met several of her fellow gardeners. They seemed like a friendly bunch, all with a common purpose to flex their green fingers as part of a small community. On Fiona's first visit, a couple in their early sixties walked over to where she was standing to introduce themselves.

'Hello there! I'm Phil and this is my long-suffering wife, Carol.'

'Pleased to meet you. My name's Fiona. Have you had your allotment a long time?'

'This is our twelfth year! We're usually down here together but sometimes I send Phil on his own, just so that I can have some peace and quiet at home!'

Carol laughed and playfully nudged her husband before continuing.

'We just had to come across and say how pleased we are that someone's going to take this plot on again. It's a bit of a mess, though.'

Fiona had to agree. The area was completely solid with a variety of weeds, although she could see the feathery green fronds of a carrot top growing near the left-hand corner.

'It'll take a lot of work but I'm up for the challenge.'

'That's the spirit! If you ever need any help or advice just come and find us. We're here every Saturday and most afternoons during the week in the spring and summer.'

'Thank you so much, both of you. You've made me feel really welcome.'

'That's O.K., dear. Of course, you're particularly lucky because you've inherited a shed, too.'

Carol's words surprised Fiona.

'Oh, I thought that belonged to the gardener opposite.'

Phil chuckled.

'No, that's yours! A bit creaky, like us after an afternoon's digging, eh, Carol?'

'Speak for yourself!'

Phil received a gentle dig in the ribs this time. He smiled warmly at his wife then explained further.

'Bert, the gardener before you, stored all his tools in there. You'll probably find everything you need and more besides. It's seen better days, mind you.'

Carol saw an opportunity to get back at her husband and happily took it.

'Look who's talking!'

The couple laughed and hugged each other, and it was clear to Fiona that their love ran deep. A question formed in her mind.

'What happened to him, Phil, if you don't mind me asking?'

'We don't really know to be honest, Fiona. He just sold up and moved away. Bert's next-door neighbour had a quick word with him the day before he left, though. Apparently, the old boy was off to start a hotel business in Torquay and looked very happy. Odd, really. He'd never mentioned wanting to do that kind of thing, and at his age!'

'How old was he?'

Phil shrugged his shoulders, but Carol said that Bert had told her he was 76. She looked up at her husband and wistfully wondered what he would be doing in *his* seventies. Phil was, in fact, contemplating the very same thing. The ensuing silence made Fiona feel slightly uncomfortable, so she decided to break it.

'Well, I think it's time to have a look, so if you'll excuse me....'

Phil and Carol, back in the present, shook Fiona's hand and left her to investigate the shed on her own.

It was in a sorry state of repair and clearly hadn't been paid any attention for many years. The flaky, blue-grey paintwork on the outside revealed weathered wood beneath, which had suffered from exposure not only to wind and rain but also to strong summer sunshine.

As Fiona looked more closely at the scarred surfaces, she noticed that a single word had been repeatedly scratched deep into the grain:

BELIEVE!

She counted at least a dozen, all created by the same hand. Slightly unnerved as to why they were there, she turned her attention to the door.

An old rusty padlock hung open-shackled and useless from the metal plate. Fiona was surprised that the shed had been left unsecured, especially as Phil had told her about the stored gardening equipment. She lifted the padlock and placed it on the ground, then forced the warped, splintered door open.

Fiona breathed in a heady mix of earthy scents in the musty atmosphere as she stepped inside. To her left was a narrow shelf stacked with terracotta flowerpots in various sizes, their exteriors shaded ghostly white with mould. Next to these were four unused seed trays, a battered watering can and a pair of gardening gloves with holes in three of the fingers. Propped in the right-hand corner were assorted garden tools, all of which appeared perfectly serviceable at first glance. On closer inspection, however, Fiona found that only the spade, hoe and trowel could be used. The handle of the fork had been snapped off at some stage in its life, and the rusted rake head came away as soon as Fiona lifted the implement clear from the rest.

She looked down at the floorboards which were covered in a mixture of soil, potting compost and long dead plant material. Fiona nudged a low-spun cobweb with her foot and dislodged a large brown spider, as surprised to be disturbed as she was to see it. She stepped back to give it space as it scuttled away to find shelter.

Fiona hadn't really noticed how many cobwebs had been created inside the shed, but now saw that almost everything was covered, to some degree, with gossamer threads. The dustier traps had been abandoned for some time, but Fiona could see that fresher ones were still inhabited.

Something caught her eye on the crowded shelf, partially obscured by the seed trays. It was a light bulb shrouded in a fine patina of dust and seemed incongruous to Fiona in those surroundings as she picked it up. This one was much larger than any household version which somewhat intrigued her. Still curious, Fiona was about to replace it when she noticed some seed packets, tucked behind a large flowerpot and further back than the light bulb had been.

Most were folded over and almost empty but there was one that felt close to full. The others bore the usual photographs of ripe fruit and vegetables, yet there was no such image on the brown paper packet. Fiona picked it up and found that someone had neatly written an odd rhyme in black across the wrinkled surface. It read:

Water until 'they' appear,
give them no more drink,
keep your mind wide open,
and prepare yourself to think.

Fiona read the strange riddle several times but could make no sense of it. The only thing she felt sure about was that it related to the package's contents, but what were 'they'? She scratched her head, put the light bulb and seeds back where she had found them and turned to go. She closed the door behind her and uttered the stranger's handwritten instructions as she left the allotment.

On the shelf behind the large flowerpot, a flickering light briefly shone from within the brown paper packet before fading slowly away. It was all beginning again.

Over the next fortnight, Fiona worked on her allotment whenever she could. By the time she had finished weeding and preparing her plot, she had met every other gardener who contentedly toiled there. Some brought gifts to welcome her such as green tomato chutney and piccalilli, made from produce grown on site, or homemade cakes. Fiona really loved the sense of community and was happy to be part of such a friendly group, and it soon became clear that a sharing culture also existed amongst the growers. Seeds and gardening tips were often exchanged, which only served to accentuate the sense of mutual respect and encouragement between them. In fact, Fiona had been given so many envelopes containing seeds from fellow gardeners that she hadn't needed to buy any.

As Fiona replaced her tools in the shed after a Saturday afternoon's planting, she remembered the near-empty packets on the shelf. She had completely forgotten about them and checked if there were any she could use. Runner beans, carrots and courgettes? No, she was already in the process of growing those, so decided to find out whether anyone else would like them. No-one was there to ask (Phil and Carol, for example, were holidaying in France), so Fiona left the seeds tucked against the window.

It was then that the package bearing the strange rhyme caught her attention. She picked it up and muttered the words several times as if reciting a kind of incantation, but to what end? The words tumbled from Fiona's lips with increasing speed and volume, and she couldn't tear her eyes away from the written instructions. The chant appeared to be in control of her thoughts, apart from one of relief that nobody was around to hear it. To her astonishment, an off-white glow started to spread from within the brown paper. The louder Fiona's recitation the brighter it became, much stronger than when it first responded to her touch after she initially left the shed. She felt a comforting warmth spread across her palms, but then the light faded and disappeared completely.

The next thing Fiona knew she was looking down at a freshly worked section of soil, with her red-handled trowel in one hand and the brown paper seed packet in the other. Hard as she tried, she could not recall having left the shed or planting the seeds, yet this had clearly taken place. Fiona read the puzzling rhyme again and realised that she still had to water them in. A real sense of purpose flowed through her as she did so, but somehow knew it came from a will other than her own.

Nothing showed itself there over the following fortnight, but then green shoots started to poke through the moist earth. Fiona still had no idea as to what 'they' might be, so kept watering the area as instructed. The leaves appeared a few days later, spreading flat upon the soil from central points. Each bore an odd pattern across its surface, raised like veins and coloured a dull red. When Phil saw them, he likened the 'design' to wiring or circuit boards. Later and on her own, Fiona recalled seeing similar impressions on dried leaves found when she swept the shed floor, but also next to one of the larger flowerpots on the shelf.

Other gardeners would wander over, look down at the unusual plants and scratch their heads in puzzlement. No-one had seen or grown anything remotely like them and they soon became the talk of the allotment.

The flat, veined leaves spread no further after a while. Gradually, interest in them started to wane as it appeared that they would bear no produce, impressive or otherwise. Fiona's attention soon turned towards harvesting her crop of vegetables which made all the weed clearance, digging and planting worthwhile. She was really happy with her first gardening season but felt slightly embarrassed that she hadn't enough produce to share with her fellow growers. This feeling was exacerbated when Phil, Carol and others insisted on giving her some of their bounty, all of which she accepted with a sheepish smile.

On a bright but chilly Sunday in autumn, Fiona decided to clear her allotment of remaining plant debris. Everything else had been removed, but she had persisted in watering the rather peculiar leaves in the vain hope that at least something might show itself. The 'circuitry' pattern still intrigued her but now the need for order took hold, so with a resigned shrug and a sigh, Fiona set her spade against the soil. She was about to press down with her left foot when she noticed something glistening in the late afternoon sunshine.

It appeared to be a round piece of glass and was situated exactly in the centre of one of the plants. On closer investigation, Fiona saw that three more globes had formed elsewhere on the plot but were less pronounced than the first. She gingerly touched the largest glass 'bud' and was startled to find that it grew slightly as a result. Curiosity won over trepidation, and Fiona pressed a finger on each of them in turn. She noticed that not only did they increase in size but also that others had formed where previously there were none.

Fiona seemed unable to break the connection with these strange forms. It was as if a current was flowing through her, and that she was an integral part of their development. Within half an hour, every glass object had revealed its fully formed shape. They were all now a uniform size and grew no further, but Fiona could see other changes taking place within them. A central stem of glass pushed upwards in each, soon followed by slender wiry growths that curled themselves into position. The most important element then appeared, namely a coiled filament secured in place between the wires. Fiona remembered from her schooldays that these are made of tungsten and have a very high melting point, and that inert gases must also be present for the whole construction to work.

'At least that's something I learnt in all those boring physics lessons!'

Amused by the thought, Fiona looked around at the allotments and saw only one other person working on their plot at the far end. Satisfied that nobody witnessed the odd occurrence, she decided nevertheless to cover the plants and their strange growths with a sheet of tarpaulin. She had been offered this during the summer by a neighbouring gardener and had stored it in her shed, thinking it might come in useful one day. Fiona found four large stones and placed one at each corner to secure the sheeting. She returned her spade to the shed, closed the door and set off for home. On the way she wondered what to do next and, more importantly, just who she could tell about what had happened without fear of ridicule.

After some consideration that evening, Fiona decided that the whole allotment community should be involved, along with Maddy and Gavin. She would host a kind of garden party, the culmination of which would be the removal of the tarpaulin. As she sent emails to all concerned (Carol had recently given her a list of contacts), Fiona imagined the look of surprise on every face at the unveiling and she could hardly wait for next Saturday.

Phil and Carol were first to arrive, followed closely by several of the allotment crowd. Some of the guests brought wine, so Phil fetched an old trestle table from his shed to accommodate everyone's contributions, including paper cups thoughtfully provided by Annie, a seasoned but quiet gardener. The atmosphere was relaxed although no-one, except Fiona, knew what was to be unveiled. She had not given anything away in her emails, which cryptically read:

SOMETHING ODD UNDER THE COVER!
BARTHOLOMEW ROAD ALLOTMENT
SATURDAY 15TH AT 6.00 P.M.

Maddy and Gavin showed up last and apologised profusely for being late, but Fiona smiled and gave them both a hug.

'I'm just so glad you could both make it. This wouldn't be the same without you.'

'What wouldn't, Fiona, and is *that* the cover you mentioned in your mysterious message?'

Maddy pointed at the olive-green tarpaulin and her sister nodded. Gavin scratched his head and looked confused.

'Well you've got a good crowd here, Fiona. I hope nobody's going to be disappointed when they see what's under there, whatever it is.'

'I'm sure they won't be, but it's getting dark so maybe I'd better start the show!'

Fiona excitedly clapped her hands a few times to get the group's attention, then paused before speaking.

'First of all, thank you for coming. Before I reveal why I've asked you here this evening, I'd just like to say a few words. To my sister Maddy, I'm so happy that you decided to move to London and that you met Gavin. It's obvious to anyone how good you are for each other.'

A gentle ripple of applause followed. Most of them knew the couple because Fiona had introduced Maddy and Gavin to several of the gardeners when she'd shown the couple her allotment, early in the tenure.

'Now for the rest of you! I really appreciate the warm welcome I've received here at Bartholomew Road. You've all been so generous with your tips and encouragement, so I wanted to share something with you, something I don't think any of you will have seen before.'

Fiona stepped towards her plot and removed each corner stone from the tarpaulin amidst a hush of anticipation. Not wishing to damage the fragile glass structures, she gently lifted the material and rolled it back slowly.

She smiled as her guests gasped in surprise, and then the questions started.

'How did you grow *those*, Fiona?'

'Wherever did you find the seeds?'

'Why didn't you tell us about them before?'

The last question came from Diane, who was usually a rather reserved woman. She had been as friendly towards Fiona as the others, albeit only for the first three months. During that time, she would sometimes wander over for a brief chat but had hardly spoken to the new gardener since. Although Fiona had sent the email invitation to the whole group, she didn't really expect to see Diane at her little event, let alone hear her ask such a curt question.

'Well, up until last Sunday there were only these rather odd leaves, Diane. I was just about to dig them up when I noticed the first glass bud, and soon every plant had a fully formed bulb at its centre.'

Fiona addressed the other questions then looked around her. She couldn't determine why, but every person appeared to be focused on a single light bulb each, with vision not straying in the slightest. She watched the silent, staring crowd for a few moments, but then noticed something happening within the bulbs themselves.

Fiona blinked twice to make sure it wasn't just her imagination working overtime. No, a flicker of light inside each bulb *had* appeared and was growing brighter by the second. As it increased, Fiona looked up and saw the intense fluorescence reflected in the eyes of her guests. They seemed to be under a kind of hypnosis, and this deeply troubled her. She felt responsible for the situation because no-one would have been there if she hadn't invited them, although no hint of danger had presented itself beforehand to persuade her to do otherwise.

Racked with guilt, Fiona looked back at the bulbs and tried to think of a way to end their luminous grip. She decided to smash them all, thus breaking the spell, and was about to turn to fetch her spade from the shed when other changes occurred.

Fiona stared as the circuit-like markings on the leaves lit up in a vibrant red, starting at their tips and moving towards the central growths. When all were illuminated, each bulb started to turn clockwise, revealing their metallic screw fittings beneath and becoming fully extended. Fiona, amazed and alarmed, realised that they were signalling their readiness to be 'harvested'.

This thought was suddenly replaced by safety concerns because each person moved towards their individual controller. Now in a state of absolute panic, especially over Maddy, Fiona started to scream out names and tugged at clothing, anything that might stop them from obeying these electrical sirens. All was to no avail, however, and a strange low hum started to emanate from the glass structures, persistent and slowly increasing. She watched helplessly as the group knelt in unison and detached the bulbs from their leafy surroundings but couldn't understand why the only people who hadn't been affected were herself and Gavin.

As one the small crowd stood upright, and Fiona watched them cradle the lit objects, still gazing at them but with a new intensity. The light and the noise grew stronger and a bond seemed to be forming between master and host, but suddenly every bulb lost power and became little more than clear glass.

The immediate area had been bathed in their full glow but now only Bartholomew Road's streetlights shone at the edges of the allotment. Fiona's guests slowly placed the large light bulbs back on the soil without a word. She noticed that the weird sound had started to fade away as had the red glow that pulsed in the leaves. She watched in amazement as each person filed past in silence, giving her a thin smile before moving towards the gates. Gavin accompanied Maddy, concerned but glad it was all over.

The stillness after the event was beautiful and the afterglow of the strong lights burned itself into Fiona's consciousness. She looked down at the collection of dulled glass on the night-shadowed plot and felt a true sense of calm. She didn't understand what had happened, let alone how or why, but suddenly realised that she had been the catalyst throughout. Rather than feeling used, her demeanour became almost serene and she smiled at each of the light bulbs in turn.

Fiona turned her attention to tidying the area before she left. She folded the trestle table and propped it against Phil's shed, then placed the empty wine bottles and paper cups in a carrier bag.

There were recycling bins close to the railings outside the allotment, so Fiona dutifully sorted the items before setting off for home. She glanced back into the darkened space and could just see the glass bulbs, their outlines now defined by moonlight as opposed to their own former brightness.

Fiona walked along Bartholomew Road, trying hard to fathom out a possible reason for the strange event. Thankfully, it appeared that no-one had been harmed during the experience, but what was the purpose of it all?

'There must be some explanation,' she muttered aloud as she turned her front door key in the lock, confusion uppermost in her mind.

The emails started to arrive the following morning. At first Fiona couldn't see any kind of pattern emerging, apart from the fact that each was sent by one of last night's attendees. After reading through them several times, however, she realised that all of them related to either life-changing plans or dreams previously unfulfilled. Barbara wrote of a desire to visit Italy to paint watercolours and that this was something she'd longed to do since her twenties. Joe, on the other hand, expressed a wish to take a road trip across America, a journey he'd put on hold for many years because of work commitments and life in general.

Annie's email was so full of enthusiasm that Fiona could scarcely believe it came from the same woman, so shy was she every time they had met on the allotment. Annie messaged that the decision to try her hand at writing novels had come 'right out of the blue' and she couldn't get plot ideas down fast enough.

An even bigger surprise came via a phone call from Phil.

'Hi, Fiona! Carol and I just wanted to thank you for the party yesterday although, to be honest, we can't remember very much about it! We've been racking our brains and all we've been able to recall is seeing lots of light bulbs on your allotment, intense light everywhere and then being back here again. Does any of that make sense to you?'

Fiona thought it best not to mention how almost everyone had knelt in a trance-like state, detached a lit bulb each and then stood motionless, staring deep into the brilliant glare.

'Not really, Phil. Nothing much happened after I removed the cover. You were all amazed by the sight of those bulbs but then, after a few more glasses of wine, people started to drift home.'

'Oh, right. That *is* strange, but it isn't the only reason for ringing. We've got something fantastic to tell you!'

Fiona would normally have been eager to share anyone's exciting news, but she had already heard from three people that morning, all bubbling with enthusiasm over their new paths in life. She tried to summon the appropriate level of interest, which proved surprisingly difficult. Fiona was never a selfish woman, yet in the back of her mind was the wish that there had been a bulb for *her*. She fully understood that her role in the experience was as facilitator and now realised what the bulbs represented, but it just didn't seem fair somehow.

'Are you still there, Fiona?'

'Yes, I'm sorry, Phil. What is it you want to tell me?'

'Basically, we both woke up this morning feeling incredibly alive! I had this idea to put to Carol and she had one of her own, and we've been chatting about them ever since. Not only that, but we're going to make them a reality!'

'That's great, Phil. What *are* these ideas of yours?'

'Well, you know Carol loves to cook, especially cakes and the like. I mean she makes pretty good pies and pasties too, but the cakes are her favourites, so we've decided to take a chance and open a café and cake shop together! My idea was the café part, but it makes perfect sense to combine the two!'

'Wonderful, Phil. Will you be moving away?'

'Hopefully not, because that empty bakery over on Ferguson Street is still up for sale. Carol used to buy her lunch there when she worked in town and says there's easily room for a few tables. We've already arranged with the agent to have a look on Monday and we're both so excited!'

'Let me know how you get on, won't you?'

'I promise, Fiona. Chat soon! Bye!'

Fiona returned the farewell and ended the call. She thought back to the delicious carrot cake that Carol had given her as a welcome to the allotment. She could almost taste the thick frosting and the delicate hint of cinnamon in the cake itself and couldn't help licking her lips at the memory.

Over the next hour three more emails arrived, each effusive and fizzing with positivity.

Penny and Graham, who recently told Fiona they'd wanted to visit New Zealand for a long time, now 'embraced the dream' and were planning a trip with a view to eventually moving there.

Nina, still in her twenties, had decided to pick up on her recently abandoned acting career. Confidence and roles had proved elusive, even though tutors had often told her she was a 'more than promising student'. Nina wrote that now she could hardly wait to show the world just what she was capable of and that this surge of inner belief would surely come across at auditions.

Sahil and Riya both worked in digital advertising but for different agencies. There was no rivalry between them, and they had often discussed setting up their own business in the field, although such conversations always ended up going nowhere. Now, however, the daunting prospect of such a venture held no fear, and the couple were actively looking at various financial ideas and arrangements.

In the afternoon, Adam excitedly rang to say that he had found the courage from somewhere to propose to Steven and that he'd said yes. Not only that, but after getting married, the couple planned to start a Bed and Breakfast business in Cornwall, something Adam had dreamed of doing for years. He was surprised and delighted to find that Steven enthusiastically embraced the idea so readily.

Fiona had a phone call from Diane in the early evening.

'I'm ringing to say that I won't be around much early next year because I've just booked a couple of spring cruises, maybe with another to follow in the summer. Terry never wanted to go on one due to his seasickness, or so he said, and I suddenly thought this morning, why not do it? It's been two years now and there's nothing to stop me, so I was wondering if you wouldn't mind looking after my patch while I'm away.'

'Of course, Diane. I won't mind at all and thank you for trusting me. I know your allotment means a great deal to you.'

'It certainly gave me something to focus on after Terry died, but suddenly I find I have a need for new adventures and experiences. I don't know where it's come from but, to be quite honest, Fiona, I feel like starting to pack already!'

Diane started to laugh. It was a high, shrill sound that just continued as if on a loop. After about a minute, Fiona decided to end the call, severing the laughter and enjoying the ensuing silence. She realised that Diane was the last of the gardeners to contact her, and that every one of them had either rekindled old dreams or sparked new ones into life, and all since yesterday's strange happenings on the allotment.

Later, whilst eating her dinner, Fiona realised that the only person who hadn't been in touch since then was Maddy. She recalled how her sister had knelt to pick up the bulb nearest her and that Gavin had remained rooted to the spot, yet as entranced as the others.

Why hadn't there been one for *him* to lift and cradle? Come to think of it, why had the number of bulbs almost exactly matched the number of people attending?

Fiona tried to convince herself that it could have just been serendipity, but somehow this explanation didn't ring true. Still puzzled, she poured herself a glass of white wine and was about to settle down for the night when her doorbell rang. When she opened the door, Maddy almost tumbled through with Gavin close behind. They flopped down onto the sofa then started laughing and whispering to each other. Fiona hated laying on the big sister routine, but somehow couldn't stop herself on this occasion.

'Are you drunk, Maddy?'

'No! Unless you mean drunk on life's possibilities, then yes, I suppose we are!'

Maddy gave her sibling a mock frown which Gavin found hilarious, and their laughter moved up a notch. Fiona stood with her arms folded and waited for them to calm down, which took several minutes. It was Maddy who spoke first.

'I'm sorry, Fiona. I can see that you're annoyed. It's just that we've got something amazing to tell you, something that could be great for all of us.'

'We're so excited about this. Please sit down and listen to what Maddy has to say.'

Fiona did as Gavin suggested and waited for Maddy to begin.

'It's about this idea I've had that's just come out of nowhere!'

A smile briefly flickered about Fiona's lips. She knew exactly where it had come from.

'Honestly, Fiona, I woke up this morning and everything made perfect sense! Look, we both know how much we miss Scotland. We used to talk about it all the time when we both lived together, and poor old Gavin has to put up with it now!'

'Yep, on and on and on she goes, and it drives me crazy!'

Gavin pretended to yawn, and his partner playfully punched him on the shoulder. They all laughed and Maddy looked across at Fiona, barely able to contain her excitement over what could amount to a new direction for all of them.

'Before I tell you my idea, Fiona, promise that you'll hear me out before you make any comments, good or bad. I haven't been able to think of anything else since the thought came to me, and the more I consider it the more sense it makes!'

Fiona earnestly promised that she would listen without interrupting, and then smiled warmly at her sister. Maddy appeared radiant with energy and her eyes were sparkling with enthusiasm, almost as if she was lit from inside, which, in effect, she was. Fiona was happy enough to indulge her sibling, but eagerness to hear what Maddy had to say turned to frustration and she could wait no longer.

'Come on, Maddy! Just tell me what this great idea is!'

'O.K. then. Here goes.'

A brief pause.

'I think we should open a Scottish pub! Think about it, Fiona. It would be fantastic! I've been looking online and there are several in central London, but none over this way so we wouldn't have any competition. As for the finance we'd need, Gavin feels pretty sure that some of his City contacts would be very interested in backing a project like this. You're going to start making enquiries when you're back at work tomorrow, aren't you?'

'I certainly am, Madds. I can already think of five potential investors, Fiona, and there are loads of pubs closing all over London, so we shouldn't have a problem finding a suitable property.'

'Gavin's right, and if we bought one that needed some renovation, it would be a great project to tackle together. Now, isn't that a great idea?'

37

Fiona slowly drank her wine and considered the proposal carefully. She could tell that Maddy wanted an affirmative answer straight away, but this was too important a decision to hurry. On the one hand both women would have to give up their current jobs, but on the other they would be working together on a very personal business venture close to their hearts. Gavin was happy to wait patiently for Fiona's response, but Maddy simply couldn't bear the tension anymore.

'Tell me what you think, Fiona! Better still, just say YES!'

'Well, the idea certainly has potential, Maddy. With Gavin's contacts and financial expertise, it stands a good chance of working and we could both contribute as well. It would be a big step for us but could be very rewarding, so it's a cautious yes from me.'

Fiona was as excited as Maddy but thought it best to appear calm and collected. In her mind she had already visualised the bar, listed half the Scottish food on the menu and decided on how often live music would be performed. Obviously, she would discuss these details with Maddy at a later stage, but for now a warm glow of anticipation swept over her.

'We should celebrate! I'll get some more glasses.'

'Oh, don't worry, Fiona. Gavin's driving and I've got an early start tomorrow. I'm just so happy that you want to be a part of this!'

They all stood and hugged each other, a tantalising future glistening in their minds. Maddy and Gavin left with a promise to come over again soon, and they waved to Fiona before they got into the car.

Fiona closed the front door and looked around her living room. The silence seemed particularly intense after such an animated discussion and she thought back to the conversation just ended. In doing so, Fiona suddenly understood the reason why no light bulb had been specifically grown for *her*. She realised that such strong familial ties with Maddy linked her to the dream, in the same way Gavin's love attached *him* to it. By standing close to Maddy as she cradled her bulb, they had shared in the moment and become inextricably linked to the one idea that would positively affect all of them.

Fiona poured another glass of wine and sat on the sofa. As she sipped the cool liquid, thoughts drifted to her shed on the allotment, its scarred, blue-grey paintwork softened by moonlight, and she imagined the door slowly opening on its own. Tucked away on the shelf behind a large flowerpot was a seed packet made of wrinkled brown paper. Through this quiet vision, she understood that the seeds themselves had determined how many she should plant, the number being completely out of her control.

After placing her empty glass on the table, Fiona stretched and smiled. It had been a fantastic day full of surprises, and she couldn't help wondering not only who would take over the plots that would soon be available, but also which dreams would light up the lives of the new intake. After all, she mused, there were at least a dozen seeds left in that packet just waiting to be planted by a lucky someone.

A year and a half on since that happy evening, we find Fiona chatting and laughing with customers. With Maddy on maternity leave, she's taken on the role of bar manager at The Stag for a while. She knows deep down that her trusted bar staff could pretty much run the place without her, although that's something she would never tell them.

A trio of fiddlers, the live band for tonight, strike up on the small stage and soon hands are clapping along to the music. It is their fourth gig at the pub, and they've proved very popular. Fiona is watching them play and is impressed by their speed and virtuosity. She is considering offering them a regular monthly slot when her thoughts are interrupted by Vicki, one of the bar staff working this evening.

'This gentleman says that the light bulb's blown in the toilet and could we fix it as a matter of urgency.'

'Of course, sir. I'll have it changed in no time.'

Fiona fetches a replacement from the store cupboard and removes the cardboard packaging. For a moment, she cradles the bulb in her hands and remembers a certain autumn evening, during which everything changed.

She leaves the office with a smile on her face, a smile as radiant as a new light bulb, in position and glowing brightly.

LAPTOP

Ellie had only written half a page all morning, and even this was deleted in frustration before she made her lunch. She shut down her laptop, closed the lid and slouched towards the kitchen. Whilst half-heartedly preparing a cheese and tomato sandwich, she acknowledged that she had taken more breaks than usual lately. Ellie felt particularly guilty regarding the half an hour she had wasted earlier just staring down at the umbrellas as they passed in the street, but what was she supposed to do? Her writer's block had lasted for five weeks now and hard as she tried, and she *had* tried, her screen remained devoid of anything of substance or worthy of development.

Ellie's most recent book, "The Whisperers in The Wall", was her most successful to date. Over three novels, she had been mining a rich seam of ideas, concerning the fortunes or otherwise of a wealthy household in the 1870s'. The Hamilton family lived a comfortable life on their large estate in Gloucestershire but were plagued by ghostly apparitions, not just in certain rooms but also in the fields and woodland nearby. During harvest time, the farm labourers often refused to come to work, especially if reports of supernatural activity were circulating amongst the villagers.

In "The Whisperers in The Wall", Ellie concentrated not so much on the imposing house as on the beautifully maintained gardens and, more specifically, one rather neglected place. The book's focus was a rather dilapidated section of garden wall, part of which ran alongside a newer and much more stable construction. Constance, the oldest of the Hamilton children, had been playing a few feet away from the old wall with her siblings one sunny afternoon. She thought she heard voices coming from somewhere and allowed her curiosity to win her over. The calls led Constance to the aged structure, and she pressed her ear to the crumbling brickwork. She was amazed, and somewhat disturbed, to hear ghosts speak directly to her, mentioning not only her parents but also relatives long dead. They told her of dark deeds committed by the family in decades past and made her promise to hold these secrets close to her heart. The wall's inhabitants knew that she would find this impossible, for Constance was nearly thirteen and thirsty for knowledge about the world around her, both past and present.

The novel focused on Constance's struggle to maintain her promise to the whisperers, and the consequences that followed when she could keep silent no longer. Ellie was particularly pleased with the double twist ending, which was as much a surprise to her loyal readership as to the writer herself when the idea first arrived.

"The Whisperers in The Wall" was a great success for Ellie but it also brought her something even more fulfilling on an intensely personal level. Callum.

Ellie first saw him in the audience at a reading and book signing arranged to promote the novel. Perhaps it was Callum's height that made him stand out in an audience some sixty fans strong, or possibly those dark brown eyes that seemed to reach inside her mind every time she met his gaze. Whatever it was Ellie felt a connection, even though this striking individual sat silently throughout the Q and A session. As she smiled during the applause at the end of the event, Ellie couldn't help hoping that she would see him in the book signing queue, waiting in turn to meet her.

She was soon sitting at the large desk provided by the bookshop. Sure enough, there he was, head and shoulders above everyone else. The closer he got to Ellie's table, the more perturbed the writer became. Her words started slurring as she spoke to each fan ahead of him, aware of a growing dryness in her throat. She gulped at a glass of water before signing another book and realised that the handsome stranger was next in line. When he stood before her, she took the copy from him and noticed that her hand was shaking.

'Who shall I sign it to?'

Her voice was as nervous as the smile she offered.

'To Callum, please. It's so good to meet you, Ellie.'

'Thank you. Would you like me to sign your other books?'

Even though Callum had all three novels with him, he only presented "The Whisperers in The Wall" to Ellie. He didn't answer her question but smiled and put a finger to his lips before turning away.

There were still around thirty fans to greet, so Ellie was soon able to refocus on the job in hand, but then she looked up into those brown eyes again. Callum presented "The Price of Deceit", her first novel, for a signature and left the desk for the second time. Corrine, the publisher's representative, watched as he returned to the back of the queue and shrugged in Ellie's direction. Nonplussed, she returned the gesture.

Callum was the last person to meet Ellie (again) when he asked for a signature on her second book. He had engineered the situation throughout the afternoon, unwittingly assisted by the fans who joined the queue after him, thus lengthening the gaps between each of his meetings with her. Now, with no more unsigned works to offer, Callum just grinned broadly at Ellie and made an appealing suggestion.

'I'm clearly your most loyal fan here today, so I was wondering if I might take you for a drink now that everyone else has gone.'

'Ms Fields has to be in Brighton tomorrow for another event so I'm afraid that won't be possible.'

Corrine had moved across to Ellie's side as if to underline the importance of sticking to their promotional schedule, but Callum persisted.

'Well let me give Ms Fields my phone number and she can text me when she's back in London, if that's alright with Ms Fields.'

Ellie's cheeks reddened and she managed to stifle a giggle. She gave Callum a tour flyer on which he wrote his details, after which he shook hands with both women and left the bookshop, turning once to flash another warm smile at the blushing novelist.

Every signing session was well attended and deemed a success, but towards the end of the run Ellie's mind kept drifting towards seeing Callum again. Ever the professional and not wishing to appear too keen, she waited a few days before texting him. He replied the same evening and a meeting was arranged for the following Saturday. Everything went perfectly over the next few dates and their relationship quickly moved from tentative to permanent.

In terms of physical characteristics alone, Callum and Ellie appeared to be a rather mismatched couple. He was 6ft 5ins tall whereas Ellie was considerably shorter at a mere 5ft 7ins. Members of the public would stare first at Callum, then at Ellie and finally at Callum again, trying to imagine their life together (or, more specifically, their sex life). They used to get upset when the same old jokes were trotted out by both family and friends, but they gradually learnt to ignore them, and the jibes tailed off as a result. After a few months, Callum and Ellie decided to buy a flat together and it is here that we find the frustrated writer on a rainy afternoon in November.

Ellie placed her empty plate in the sink, leant against the kitchen doorframe and looked around the room. She had initially disliked the bright yellow walls and spoke to Callum of a possible need to redecorate. His persuasive manner, however, convinced her that she should 'live with it for a while' and that she might change her mind as a result. She smiled, acknowledging that the colour contrasted beautifully with her Mexican wall plaques in shades of orange, cobalt and red. He was right after all.

Ellie resumed her seat at the table and lifted the lid of her laptop. She pressed the 'on' button, and suddenly found herself plagued by doubts over what happened to her old machine. Deep down Ellie was pretty sure that Callum hadn't damaged it deliberately. Besides, why would he? Their love was strong, and she had no real reason to question his account of the incident. Ellie tried to convince herself that it must have been an accident. There was no other explanation, although....

Ellie had been out for a long walk, looking for a sliver of inspiration somewhere, *anywhere* that could break the creative deadlock. As soon as she opened the front door, Callum had rushed towards her and held her close. He loosened his embrace and looked down into her confused eyes.

'Ellie, Ellie, my love. I'm so sorry and I promise I'll buy you a new one this week.'

'Buy me a new what?'

She managed to push him away and saw her laptop on the kitchen table, its screen heavily cracked and the casing damaged. Ellie rounded on her partner, awaiting an explanation.

'Look, I came home early and thought I'd give you a nice surprise by cooking something special this evening. You've been so stressed lately over your writing and you know I want to help in any way I can. When I found you weren't here, I got so worried and I knocked your laptop onto the floor in a state of panic. I'm truly sorry.'

Ellie wanted to believe him. He certainly appeared contrite, but something didn't quite ring true. She looked down at the ruined glass, doubting whether a simple fall from table to wooden floor could have had such an impact. It appeared much more likely to her that the device had been dashed against the boards with some force, and from a considerable height. Her documents were kept in the cloud storage system, so nothing was lost. She had written her best work on this laptop, however, so it had attained a sentimental status over time.

True to his word, Callum bought a new laptop two days later. It was such a beautiful sleek object that Ellie almost forgave him for the damage inflicted on her old one. Almost.

It took no time at all for her to get used to the new piece of equipment, and she was impressed by the speed and simplicity of operation. If only she could think of something to write on it, she ruefully observed each morning, as the blank screen mockingly stared back at her. Ellie's publishers, delighted with the success of "The Whisperers in The Wall", had expressed their eagerness for her to start the next book as soon as possible. She was asked at a recent meeting what the next novel would be about and had avoided answering the question directly, offering only a vague outline of a plot she had abandoned some time ago.

Ellie's desperation had increased dramatically in the last few days, to the extent that she felt a need to research techniques to end writer's block. In amongst tips such as listening to classical music or talking to an imaginary friend was a suggestion to feel as comfortable as possible before attempting to write anything. Ellie slipped off her socks in order to try this and placed her bare feet upon the hard, wooden flooring.

There was one element of the replacement machine that always distracted Ellie but in a good way, for each time she prepared to log on a fascinating photograph would appear. Whether the image was a snow-capped mountain range, a mass of brightly coloured balloons or a shot of the Grand Canyon, they caused her to pause and study every picture in detail. It was only when she had to face the unforgiving whiteness of the empty screen again that her heart would sink as before, and she longed to be somewhere else.

Now, as Ellie prepared to enter her password, she wondered whether an alternative might more accurately reflect her current situation. She considered LiteraryFraud, CreativelyDead1 or even HateCallum4ever, realising that she still didn't quite believe him regarding what happened to her beloved laptop. She was so lost in her continuing inner torment that she hardly noticed the new imagery before her. On this occasion, a stunningly beautiful garden met her eyes and she could barely believe that such a wondrous place existed, other than in someone's fantasy.

The first thing Ellie noticed was the wall that ran across the garden, effectively slicing the photograph in two. This one was very different to the crumbling red brick construction featured in her last novel, formed as it was of tightly laid cobblestones. Beyond the wall lay rolling green hills, and in the distance to the right was a ruined yet still imposing castle. The sky was cloudless, and a shade of blue Ellie found hard to accurately define, eventually deciding that the best description was a palette mix of cobalt, ultramarine and turquoise.

Ellie cast her eyes to the amazing floral display in the foreground and the almost dizzying range of colours. Some plants she didn't recognise but in the main they were familiar to her, although even these seemed strange somehow. It was as if every bloom had been spray-painted a few tones brighter than normal, and Ellie found this vibrancy increasingly disturbing. She looked away from the screen but could not resist returning her gaze to such a captivating image.

The garden had completely absorbed Ellie's mind and she started to wonder what the array of flowers might smell like. She imagined that the amalgam of so many heady scents would be extremely pleasurable to experience, but also almost suffocating in its intensity.

Every element of the photograph tugged at her curiosity. She wanted to walk across the hills and explore the castle ruins, run her hands over the rough surface of the wall on her return then walk amongst the flowers, joyfully taking in their wondrous perfumes. The longing to be within the frame became an all-consuming desire, and she could not turn away as before. Her eyes darted around the screen with increasing rapidity as if she was desperately trying to find a way in, a visual key or clue that would admit her entry somehow.

Ellie's frustration ended when she was met by a memory. It concerned a plot device she had utilised in her second novel "Ask Not the Mirror", in which an old superstition within the Hamilton household became a reality. The book centred on the ornate mirror in the main hallway of the large house. The object was imposing and, when the children were young, they would run past it rather than catch their faces in the scratched glass. The frame, which was covered in curlicues, possessed a weathered beauty and was difficult to ignore.

No-one could say with any certainty where the object came from but, as far back as anyone could remember, a curse had been associated with it and was always taken seriously. Every child had been told to heed the warning not to ask the mirror anything concerning the family's past or future, or they would surely rue the day.

What nobody remembered was that there was originally a second part to the hex, namely that a hand should never be placed upon the mirrored surface whilst asking the question. This element revealed itself when Robert, a visiting cousin, stood before the looking glass as a dare set by Henry, the middle Hamilton child. Robert stared at his reflection and made his enquiry but felt bidden to simultaneously place his hand upon the mirror. Henry, who had been giggling throughout, watched in horror as his relative quickly faded into thin air before his eyes, never to be seen again.

Although not a resounding success, "Ask Not the Mirror" was well received and helped Ellie to establish herself as a respected writer. Now, however, she felt the same urge to touch the glass as her character had experienced, a need deep within that was impossible to explain or understand. She moved her left hand towards the screen and placed her palm flat against it. Ellie closed her eyes for a few moments and couldn't quite believe what she saw when she opened them again.

Bright yellow walls. Her Mexican wall plaques. The rain spattered window. Ellie's hand was still pressed against the glass only now she was on the other side, looking back into the room. She removed her hand from the screen and slowly turned around, ready to feast her eyes on the fabulous garden.

The vista was even more astonishing than when Ellie saw it from the lounge, bored and creatively barren on yet another grey November afternoon. The flowers were as radiant as she remembered them, but now they positively shimmered before her. Red, yellow and orange blooms were set against dark purples and blues, all accentuated further by the verdant glossiness of their leaves. Their unsettling brightness forced Ellie to close her eyes every so often, and she felt a certain dizziness each time she reopened them.

Whilst sitting at her laptop Ellie had tried to imagine the collective garden fragrances, but nothing conjured in her mind came anywhere near the reality. Every scent she had ever known seemed to be vying for her attention, merging in the sultry air to form new alliances. Ellie had longed to experience this aspect on the other side of the screen, but the cloying sweetness was overwhelming, and she wanted to escape it somehow.

With this goal in mind, Ellie looked past the captivating floral display to the garden wall and what lay beyond. She felt a deep desire to be walking barefoot through the soft grass and then on to the castle ruins, thoroughly intrigued by the ancient building. She tried to imagine what the stronghold would have looked like when it was in use but had to admit that the abandoned fortress now displayed a kind of decrepit majesty all of its own.

Ellie looked down and saw a moss-laden path that led to the garden wall. She could not determine exactly where it started, due to the abundant foliage that completely covered the ground where she stood. As her eyes followed the paving, she was surprised to find that there was no sign of a gate set into the cobbled structure. Maybe Ellie imagined it, but the entangling perfumes in the air suddenly intensified. They caught in her throat and she started to cough uncomfortably. The need to reach the hills and castle grew stronger within her, so she decided to leave the garden behind, even if it meant clambering over the wall in the process.

Placing a hand over her mouth, Ellie set her left foot upon the path which triggered an odd transformation. The moss around the paving stones started to turn from dark green to a dry brown, before changing further to a paler hue. Confused, she took a few more steps, brushing against several of the beautiful plants as she did so (it would have been impossible to do otherwise, as some of the blooms bowed over the pathway). Those she touched instantly began to wither and droop, and she watched in sadness as their petals fell to the ground, leaving only decomposing flower heads behind. The disease began to infect every plant in the garden, if anything spreading faster as it moved further towards the wall.

Ellie stood still amidst a sea of rotting leaves and blackened blooms. The mixture of wonderful fragrances, initially enjoyed but later endured, had been replaced by a powerful stench of foul decay. Through her astonishment at what was happening, Ellie had lifted her hand from her face, but now replaced it in order to stop her stomach heaving over the disgusting odour.

She ran towards the garden wall and placed her hands atop the cobbled surface, ready to clamber over and leave the scene of devastation behind. As with the plants, however, everything turned to ruin and she watched in horror as every stone collapsed in on itself, leaving only grey dust at her feet.

With her view now unencumbered, Ellie looked towards the castle in the distance. She found some comfort in its solid structure, certain that it would not succumb to the strange affliction, seemingly brought about by her mere presence in the garden. Ellie's hopes soon disintegrated as she watched the rolling hills in the foreground yield to the peculiar metamorphosis, each blade of grass withering and immediately affecting its neighbour. Next to surrender was the sky, the stunning blue leaching first to a leaden grey then on to a solid, unforgiving black.

The plague inevitably reached the castle, but nothing happened immediately, which gave Ellie time to consider all that had taken place since her arrival. She wondered how long she had been there, and if the concept of time even existed in such an odd environment. These thoughts were superseded by a question:

Would she ever find a way back to the bright yellow room and her familiar life with Callum?

Ellie decided that she wouldn't doubt her partner's word again if she *did* return to the ordinary world, instead appreciating his kindness and support. A sudden mixture of loneliness and panic engulfed her, and tears soon fell upon the putrid mass at her bare feet. She watched as even these impacted the ground, bursting into small flames before dying away moments later. Ellie was forced from her misery by a rumbling sound in the distance. She looked towards the castle and watched as a single crack spread up from the ground, before five fissures branched from it giving the impression of a skeletal hand, effortlessly claiming the ruin.

Ellie cried out as the masonry started to fall onto the ravaged hills. The ancient structure was the last vestige of normality to surrender to the chaos around her, and she stood motionless, surveying the damaged landscape. The only movement was a light breeze that spread the fetid stink to all four corners of the image.

Still standing where the wall had been, Ellie's thoughts turned to getting away from what was once such a beautiful garden, its demise somehow caused by her arrival. As she struggled to focus on a plan, invisible hands grabbed her shoulders and spun her around to look towards the glass screen, now completely smeared with botanical decay and foul detritus. Before Ellie could work out what was happening, the same hands aggressively pushed her forwards with such force that she fell onto the slime and filth.

She was immediately hauled to her feet, and frog marched towards the point of her entry. Ellie's transparent assailant started to speak in a language she couldn't understand, spitting out the words with pure venom and hatred. The speech was punctuated by intermittent barks and hisses, which served to underline how unwelcome Ellie was there.

When they reached the laptop glass, the spectre stopped speaking but maintained its powerful grip on Ellie's arms. With no warning, it used a third hand to push her face against the stained surface, whilst a fourth grabbed at her hair.

There was no doubt. She had clearly violated the creature's space, contaminating it with human curiosity and the inherent need to explore. As Ellie screamed in terror, she realised that everything in the garden and beyond would return to its former glory once she found a way back to the other side, but how? She frantically darted her eyes back and forth in a desperate attempt to find some mark, some symbol that would help her escape but there was nothing. The garden's guardian started to scream into her left ear and forced her head down so that she had to look at the ground. It kicked away some of the rotten vegetation and, in doing so, revealed Ellie's fate.

The area was littered with human skulls and many bones to accompany them. There was no way back after all. Every man or woman who entered this place had died here, tormented by the custodian's wrath. Ellie managed to raise her head and stared at the dirty window to her world. Peering through the murk, she thought she could see the door opening in the room beyond. With sheer determination, she managed to wrest one arm free and wiped a large space clean. Ellie, panic stricken, watched as Callum entered the flat and took off his coat and scarf.

Although she couldn't hear what he was saying to himself, his actions made perfect sense to her. Ellie watched as Callum mockingly typed on the keyboard, then pretended to rub at his eyes and cry imaginary tears. He soon got bored with his game and stared at the blank screen for a while. With a face full of bitterness and envy, Callum dashed the laptop onto the floorboards with one violent movement and stormed into the kitchen.

Now fully aware of her partner's *real* reaction to her writing hiatus, Ellie formed her hands into fists and started beating on the glass with increasing frustration. The machine lay open on the floor so the imprisoned author thought that escape might still be possible, not realising that every strike against the screen brought the laptop nearer to a shut position. The lid silently closed, signalling Ellie's death in the other world, and the keeper of the garden let out a single howl of victory. It could hardly wait to begin the restorative process and revelled in the opportunity provided by the intrusion to create new plants with even stronger colour and perfume.

Callum was sure the laptop hadn't fallen closed when he knocked it from the table. He sat down and ate his sandwich, barely giving Ellie a second thought. I loved her once, he considered, but all that recent angst over not being able to start the next book about that bloody Hamilton family had been too much to stomach.

He picked up his mobile phone and rang Naomi.

'Hi, babe. Looks as if she's gone out so I can come over. Probably be able to stay the night, yeah? After all, the self-important bitch hardly notices when I'm around these days.'

'You deserve better, much better, and I'm sure you know what I mean. Anyway, see you in…. twenty minutes?'

'I'm leaving right now. Can't wait to hold you again, Naomi. Bye!'

'Me too, lover. Bye!'

Callum ended the call and smiled knowingly to himself. He had no intention of taking a shower. Naomi liked to sniff at his sweat-stained, workaday shirt as she undressed him, and who was he to complain? Their little 'arrangement' was working well for both parties and neither saw any reason to close it down.

After picking up his car keys, Callum nonchalantly looked around the room. He gave the laptop a heavy kick which sent it scudding to the skirting board where it lay forlorn and unwanted. He grabbed a bottle of white wine from the fridge on a whim, slammed the front door shut and hurried down the stairs, already imagining the pleasures of the evening, and night, ahead.

Over the next few months, Ellie Field's readership would increasingly wonder what happened to their favourite novelist. Eventually, following the police inspector's inevitable television statement that the search for Ms Fields was being called off and that Mr. Callum Anderson was to be released without charge, her fans would console themselves by re-reading her trio of novels. Each would be sorely disappointed that they would never meet members of the Hamilton family again, especially Constance, who first heard the garden wall whispering to her.

The garden wall in the other place was the first element to be restored. It took only moments to reconstruct, each cobblestone reforming from the grey dust due to intense magic produced by the invisible entity. Every stone positioned itself in the same place as before, solid evidence that balance and order were returning. Towards the back of the garden, the creature kicked aside Ellie's lifeless body, ready for replanting to commence. It looked up and watched as the first patches of grey broke through the black, satisfied that a blue of almost indescribable beauty would soon burst across the sky once again.

GNOME NOT SO SWEET GNOME

You move through the automatic doors, pass by the gormless looking sales assistants into the overly twee gift shop area, then walk briskly past the little jars of Granny Someone-or-other's Fig and Ginger Chutney, complete with their red gingham lid covers (the whole produced on an industrial estate in somewhere like Slough or Swindon and nowhere near a country cottage). You try to convince yourself that driving for just under an hour to look at overpriced comestibles is a valid use of your Sunday morning. Once you've failed miserably in this endeavour, you stroll through the section of brightly coloured watering cans which are far too small to water *anything* successfully even if filled to the brim.

You ignore the plastic flower display to your left and the range of cute animal ornaments to your right (yes, that owl's eyes really *do* seem to follow you everywhere) and quell the need to scream out loud that you haven't seen a single living plant yet.

You reach the doors that lead to the nursery, but as you step outside you can already see many more examples of expensive tat and nonsense ahead. Several classical Greek figures have been plonked unceremoniously next to large Buddhas, displaying protruding stomachs in stark contrast to their athletically built neighbours. Close by is a veritable menagerie of gaudily painted creatures, from both the natural and mythological worlds. Fierce dragons, mouths agape, vie for space with stern looking herons and oversized squirrels.

Beyond these you see some actual plants (at last!) so you move towards them, eager to leave the unattractive statuary behind, but there are yet more ornaments further along the path.

You pause at the highly glazed globes and acknowledge that some of the blue ones are quite attractive, but the next display cancels out any desire to purchase *anything* here.

There are twelve of them, standing in a row like rosy-cheeked sentinels, each with one hand raised in greeting. You wonder why the gesture strikes you as menacing and realise that you've interpreted the collective as a secret society gathering and that this is a coded message to all those involved. With their bright blue jackets and scarlet hats, these jolly, white-bearded figures have always struck you as the epitome of bad taste, and these extra-large ones only serve to reinforce that opinion. In fact, so disgusted are you by their fake bonhomie and sickly-sweet characterisation (as well as the price tag of £60 each) that you decide to leave the garden centre immediately, angry that there appear to be more expensive distractions than plants in this place.

'Damn! That was a close one.'

'What do you mean, No. 3? Barely looked at us before storming off. It's only when they spend a while standing in front of us that they decide to make a purchase. Haven't you realised that yet?'

'Give him a chance, No. 8! He only took over from the last No. 3 yesterday. Now *that* was a close one! It nearly wasn't a sale at all. That couple took ages to make their minds up and it was only when their little girl started crying that they bought him.'

'He'll have lots of fun there, causing accidents and general mayhem.'

'Yes, and her parents will never work out why their sweet little girl becomes increasingly bitter and angry towards them!'

'Agreed, No. 10, but don't get so excited. You're trembling at the prospect, which is understandable, but we don't want to give ourselves away, do we?'

'Sorry, No. 1. I'll stay completely still from now on.'

'Very good. Even though our victims can't hear our conversations, we must be careful regarding movement. Besides we need to set an example for our new No. 3.'

'Agreed, No. 1.'

'No. 5 is very quiet today. Come to think of it, he's been quiet for a while now.'

'Are you surprised, No. 7? I mean, that family picked him up and put him back three times last week before just walking away. It's enough to make anyone's heart sink.'

'If we had hearts.'

'Which we certainly *don't*....'

'That's funny, No. 12!'

'Right, settle down! Potential hosts approaching, so no sudden movements, everyone!'

'Ah, it's an elderly couple. I like them because they're easy to influence once they're standing before us, and they always think we're *so* cute!'

'If only they realised, No. 4.'

'But where would be the fun in that, No. 6?'

'True, true.'

'Look, they've stopped and they're both smiling. That's always a good start.'

'Indeed, No. 2. They're closest to you, No. 4. Tell us what they're saying.'

'Well, he just told her that it *is* her birthday present, so the price doesn't matter.'

'IT? They'll be sorry for referring to us in such a way. Carry on, No. 4. What else?'

'She thinks it might be.... a bit too big for their small garden, but he thinks it would work well as an amusing focal point.'

'Let's see how amusing they think the focal point is when one of them has a nasty fall in the garden, brought about by yours truly!'

'What makes you think they'll choose you, No. 6? It could be any of us.'

'I'm pretty sure it won't be *you*, No. 9. The damage to your left boot sustained when that idiot dropped you the other day hardly makes you first choice, does it?'

'You *know* I've tried to will various staff members to paint over the scratches several times, but they seem immune. I mean, we all know how ridiculously easy it is to manipulate the human mind, but not this batch. It doesn't even work when they're bending close after bringing out a fresh replacement. I don't understand it.'

'Maybe they're just too thick to penetrate.'

'That's an unwelcome comment, No. 11. After all, it is they who unwittingly perpetuate our evil deeds by maintaining our stock levels. We should thank them for their support rather than resorting to insults. Besides, you're bound to be chosen one day, No. 9.'

'Yeah, by someone with poor eyesight.'

'That's enough, No. 12! I think we're close to a decision here....'

'They're going for.... you, No. 5! Look - the old fool's reaching down to pick you up!'

'Let's not be hasty, No. 4. Remember what happened to him last week.'

'This feels different, everybody! They're doing such a thorough inspection of my paintwork that I'm *sure* this is my turn!'

'He's looking at her and smiling, and yes.... there it is, she's kissed him on the cheek! Result!'

'You're on your way, No. 5! After your recent disappointment, feel free to be as vengeful as you like with these two. Maybe even kill one of them. It's all up to you now!'

'Sing our chant as I leave you, my brothers!'

'Of course, No. 5. Do your very worst!'

'I will! Goodbye!'

'Ready, everyone? MALEVOLENT NEVER BENEVOLENT! MALEVOLENT NEVER BENEVOLENT! MALEVOLENT NEVER BENEVOLENT!'

RECULTIVATION

An unappreciated gift ('Whatever made him think I'd want to read *that*?'), having been deliberately stained with cold coffee ('It really *was* an accident!'), will be placed in a carrier bag with others destined for the charity shop ('I'm sure someone will buy them, don't worry!'). Similar loads from similar households will be carelessly packed and dumped outside closed premises on the high street, barely protected from the early morning drizzle. Later, after warming cups of tea or coffee, staff will take out the donated items in the back room, knowing that a large proportion will be of no value whatsoever. They will find some with ripped pages and others with complete pages missing. There will be those defaced with crayon, marker or poster paint, the results of a combination of bored children and rainy afternoons.

On a different scale entirely but towards the same end, publishing houses that operate on a 'returns' basis will arrange for covers to be removed from unsold merchandise and sent back to them as evidence that the books' 'innards' have been destroyed, discarded or recycled into other products. The publisher will then present the detached covers to the bookseller for refund on the wholesale book deal.

Whether unloved or unread, defiled or dumped, each of these books will eventually end up at a pulping facility, and it is at one such site in southern England where something strange has been noticed.

'Hey, Jim! Look at this!'

'What is it, mate? Come on, it's nearly home time and I've had enough for today!'

Jim, with his mind focused on a steak and kidney pie and a couple of pints, tries to ignore his rumbling stomach and walks over to where his colleague of twelve years is standing. Roy points at something small and black, situated at the base of one of the paper stacks delivered earlier that day.

'That wasn't there this morning.'

'What? It's just a weed, Roy, nothing else.'

'No, look. It's coming out of the paper itself, and when did you last see a weed with black leaves?'

'And when did you last take an interest in plants? I suppose it is a bit odd now you mention it, but let's go, mate. I'm starving!'

The two men walk back to the main building, happy that their shift is over and barely give the strange seedling another thought.

Everything starts to change around midnight. The small plant begins to stretch and curls upwards, its stem thickening as it climbs. Within only minutes, it develops a rope-like twist and more dark leaves break out along its now considerable length. Soon more vines grow close to the base of the paperbacks, effortlessly entwining with the first. Tendrils emerge and link with each other, providing an even tighter grip on the unwanted books, but these are more than just unwanted. The cover-stripped volumes in *this* pile are especially bad in both plot and execution, and herein lies the reason for the botanical growth's existence.

By sheer coincidence, every work in the stack is almost an affront to literature and needs to be more than just pulped. For instance, there are sixteen copies of a detective story in which the identity of the murderer is virtually given away in the fourth chapter, rendering the remainder of the story almost pointless. Underneath these are twenty editions of a romantic novel. This effort is so banal and inconsequential that any reader a few chapters in would be crying out for a rampant, no-holds-barred sex scene, just to make the mind-numbingly boring characters feel or do *something* other than stare dreamily into each other's eyes. The bland leading the bland, so to speak.

Elsewhere in the stack but in complete contrast, are eighteen copies of a science fiction story based on the familiar concept of time travel. The plot of this book, however, is incredibly convoluted and far-fetched, making it virtually impossible to follow. Anyone trying to understand the various machinations weaving throughout the tale would surely grow increasingly annoyed, hurling the book against the wall in sheer frustration before reaching the half-way point. Other books now held fast by the writhing plants include wildly inaccurate historical novels and autobiographies of 'celebrities', their careers already fading.

As one, the roping vines tighten their grip on the unloved volumes and another change takes place. At the top of each plant a bud appears, rapidly swelling and ready to burst into bloom in a matter of minutes. They all open at the same time, huge and sunflower-like, but these heads are black and barely visible in the pale moonlight, twisting atop their thick stems as if searching for something.

The climbers take this as a signal to squeeze their captives even tighter, to such an extent that thousands of words start to flood out from the top of the stack. They stream in long, elegant flows into the night air, arching high before starting to descend. The flowers, their purpose clear and determined, position themselves to receive each nutrient source and eagerly feast on every syllable. These plants have invented a garden of sorts, not directly cultivated by humans but formed from some of their imaginations, albeit not particularly creative ones.

The black petals detach themselves from every bloom, leaving a circular mass of seeds on each head. With the assistance of the pliable stems, they fall face down onto the constricted paper ready to discharge their cargo into the stack's centre. All the seeds detach themselves and immediately burrow into the blank pages, setting words against each other in new arrangements. When the frenzy of intense literary activity ends and the paper has finished forming new shapes, the remaining vines wither away as they fall to the concrete.

Where once stood a pile of unloved books now stand two piles of neatly collated manuscripts, fresh and unattributed. The first is entitled "A Death in the Future" and concerns a story about a time-travelling detective with a deeply personal grudge, the denouement of the story well concealed until the last few pages. The second is called "Lust Across the Centuries" and tells of an erratic, erotic entanglement between a historical figure and a lifelike android, past and future occasionally merging together. Both novels have an unexpected twist thrown into the mix, certain to engage readers to the very end.

From dumped paperbacks denuded of their covers, new works have emerged with thoroughly engaging characters and greatly improved storylines. All they need now is someone to discover them, read them and claim them as their own. The first pages of the top copies are gently lifted by a night breeze that rises and falls intermittently, as they wait in the soft moonlight for dawn to arrive.

'I bloody hate early shifts, especially after doing a late the previous day. It's hardly worth going to sleep, is it?'

'I know what you mean, Jim. If I hadn't set the alarm last night, I'd still be in bed now.'

It's 7.20 a.m. and Roy and Jim have stepped outside for a smoke before starting work, well away from the paper stacks in the yard but close enough for Roy to notice that something appears to be missing. He holds a hand up to shield his eyes from the sun's early morning dazzle then nudges his colleague's arm.

'That gap wasn't there yesterday, was it, Jim? I'm sure we had a complete row when we finished off last night.'

'We did, mate, but we haven't now. Come on.'

The two men extinguish their cigarettes in the unit provided then walk towards what appears to be a space in the line, discovering the neatly stacked piles of paperwork moments later.

'Well I'll be....'

They look at each other in confusion and amazement. Roy picks up the top copy of "Lust Across the Centuries" and encourages Jim to do the same with "A Death in the Future". After flicking through the pages and reading random paragraphs, they swap manuscripts. Even though their shifts are about to start, the stories are so completely engaging that the real world temporarily loses its grip on their minds. Roy and Jim sink deeper into their respective fantasy worlds, now barely acknowledging each other's presence, and it is only when someone shouts to them from the main building that they return to the ordinary again.

Roy notices that his cover bears only the title and draws this to Jim's attention.

'There's no name on mine either, mate. That's odd!'

The shouts continue from the doorway, now littered with some rather colourful expletives, but the longstanding colleagues simply choose to ignore them. Roy offers Jim a cheeky grin which he returns, and it is quite clear that the same commercial thought has occurred to both men.

'I always wanted to write a book you know.'

'Me too, mate, me too.'

Jim sees a heavy-duty sack nearby and runs to fetch it, shouting to their increasingly angry supervisor that they'll 'only be a few more minutes'. He returns to Roy and they laugh conspiratorially as they hurriedly push every copy inside, amounting to fifty in all. Roy grabs the sack and rushes with it to the nearby car park, whilst Jim moves towards the plant, ready to offer an explanatory lie about the 'missing' paper stack ('I've no idea where it's gone, Jeff. It's an odd thing to nick, but there's some funny people about these days....').

They find it extremely difficult to maintain even a semblance of interest during the shift, both aware that the prospect of a much more interesting career lies tantalisingly within their grasp. Roy and Jim celebrate this potentially exciting development after work, but an element of realism creeps into the conversation.

'Of course, we've only got one book each so that's not going to be enough.'

'Look, Roy. We've both read enough from them to know they're bloody good. If…. when they take off, I reckon we could cobble together similar plotlines for another three at least! Jane's always telling me that's what her favourite authors do, and they seem to get away with it, so what do you say?'

Roy pauses for a few moments. Over the last two years, he's been longing to find a way out of his boring job at the plant. He has discussed it with Jim on several occasions, during which his colleague has expressed the same need to escape. He stares deep into his half empty glass, then looks up and gives his answer.

'I don't know what happened in the yard last night, but I *do* know we'd be crazy not to follow this through. The kids are making their own way in the world now and neither of us have any financial worries. Besides, we both retire in a couple of years, so I say let's go for it!'

'Brilliant, mate! Jane and Brenda will think we've gone mad at first, but when they read the manuscripts they'll be as excited as we are!'

Jim orders another round (Roy, ever responsible, has been on soft drinks as he's driving) and the two friends laugh and joke about not having to put up with Jeff for much longer.

'I never could stand him, Roy. He always leaps on any little mistake and tells you off like you're back at school!'

'Exactly, Jim, and it's not as if he's great at his *own* job. Those security cameras have been out of action for over a fortnight now and he's barely looked at them, let alone got them fixed!'

There are only three vehicles in the pub car park, one of which is Roy's hatchback. In the boot, held in a sack and covered over with an old tartan blanket lie two manuscripts, twenty-five copies of each. So far, only two people have read parts of them, but in a matter of time many will enjoy these novels and will eagerly await subsequent works by both authors.

The plant will continue to mash and pulp as usual, overseen by the over-officious Jeff. One thing is certain. No copies of "A Death in the Future" or "Lust Across the Centuries" will find their way back to the concrete yard where they were created under pale moonlight. Literary equilibrium has been restored.

MR. JONES

'But you only went over to the grave on Tuesday, Jean. Why do you want to go again?'

Jean settled her teacup back in its saucer and ate the last mouthful of ginger cake, unsure as to how to answer her friend's well-meaning question.

'To be honest I don't know, Muriel. I just feel a need somehow, as if I'm being nudged to go back there. Does that make any sense to you?'

'Look, we've known each other for over 40 years, and I know how hard it's been for you to cope since you lost Jack. Len died nearly twelve years ago, and I miss him as much now as I ever did. Sometimes I *still* think he's going to step into the kitchen from the garden, whistling that annoying little tune of his and asking if I want a cuppa. I'd give anything to hear those notes again, just one last time.'

'He really loved that garden, didn't he?'

'He did. Len was always out there, even when it was raining hard. All those times I shouted down the garden for him to come inside! I can see myself now, telling him that if he doesn't put down that spade, he'll catch his death....'

An awkward silence spread across the table and neither woman knew what to say or how to break it. Instead they both stared out of the café window and, by way of distraction, watched people going about their daily business on a typical afternoon in late August. Stressed parents, happy that the school holidays were nearly at an end, caved into demands for ice-cream yet again. Besuited businessmen ached to get home and take cool showers in order to feel human, rather than remain the snarling, sweaty beasts they had tetchily become throughout the day.

The two ladies looked away from the window at the same time, their eyes meeting only briefly before gazing downwards. Muriel watched as Jean absentmindedly pushed the cake crumbs around her plate with a teaspoon, then reached across to touch her friend's hand in reassurance.

'What I was trying to say was that you'll always miss Jack, and don't let anyone tell you that it gets easier because it doesn't, but you'll learn to enjoy your memories and they *will* sustain you. Besides, it's only five months since the funeral, so everything's bound to feel raw and strange.'

Jean managed a half-smile and Muriel took her hand away, suddenly curious about one aspect of their conversation.

'You said you felt nudged to visit Jack's grave again. What exactly did you mean?'

'It's almost like I'm being called there, yet at the same time told to wait. I've never experienced anything like this before, Muriel, and I wish I wasn't now.'

'Perhaps it's just because your loss is so recent, Jean. Grief can affect people in very different ways, especially the early stages.'

'I've thought of that, but this feels as if it's connected with someone *else's* pain. There's a sense of being detached and involved at the same time.'

Muriel struggled unsuccessfully to understand Jean's last comment, concerned both by her friend's words and the confused look on her face, so decided to take charge of the situation.

'Right! I'll just go and pay, then we can take a stroll through town for a spot of window shopping. Hopefully that will help to ease your worries, for a little while at least.'

'Thank you, Muriel. You're a good friend.'

Jean watched as Muriel stood and walked to the counter, happy to have such a trustworthy companion and confidante. She had hoped that through telling her about these odd

69

sensations they might start to recede, but they were becoming harder to ignore, even now. It wasn't that she was hearing voices or internal commands. No, these thoughts possessed a certain subtlety, yet were increasingly demanding her attention.

Muriel slid the change into her purse and fixed a warm smile before turning around and walking back to the table. Jean mirrored the expression and wondered what her friend was really thinking about the strange revelation. They left the café in silence but were soon engaged in general conversation again, encouraged by the warm sunshine.

'Hello?'

'Jean, it's Muriel. I just had to ring and tell you.'

'Tell me what?'

'I've started to feel the same as you. About visiting the graveyard, I mean.'

'Well that's weird. Are you sure?'

'Yes. Nothing unusual happened since we met up last week, but this morning I found myself staring at the coat rack in the hall, as if I needed to prepare to go somewhere. The image of Len's grave suddenly flashed across my mind and then everything went back to normal. Is that what happens to you, Jean?'

'Not exactly, although on Thursday I looked down and discovered I'd put my best shoes on without remembering when or why. The need to go there has been getting stronger, Muriel, and now you're experiencing similar things I'm getting a little scared.'

'I have to admit it's all a bit peculiar, but at least now I can understand what you've been going through, Jean. What I find particularly strange is that this calling, or whatever it is, doesn't feel threatening in any way. It just wants to be acknowledged and acted upon for some reason.'

It was as if the line had gone dead at this point, neither woman knowing what to say next. To end the awkwardness, Jean eventually asked a question.

'When are you thinking of visiting Len's grave, Muriel?'

'This sounds really odd, Jean, but I get a strong sense that I'll be told when to go there, and that I must wait for now.'

'Yes, I mentioned that in the cafe! I wonder if other people are having these thoughts.'

'Give me a ring if you hear of anyone else, Jean, and I promise I'll do the same. Oh, there's someone at the door. We'll chat soon. Bye!'

'Bye!'

No-one had rung Muriel's doorbell. The thought of this seemingly morbid desire and its possible spread unnerved her, so much so that she didn't want to discuss the matter further, even with her best friend. Had she known it to be a lie, Jean would have understood the reason for its existence. She sat in the hallway deep in contemplation long after the phone call had ended, trying to work out why this was happening and what it all meant, but to no avail.

It was true. The only option was to wait.

Jean wasn't at all surprised when she saw Muriel walking up the path in her best outfit. She had spent the morning trying to decide what *she* should wear, having received the 'instruction' to visit the graveyard that afternoon.

Five days had passed since their last phone call. During that time, no-one in their social circle had mentioned a need to go there, a point raised by Jean as soon as she ushered Muriel in and closed the front door.

'Do you think it really is just us, Muriel? Are we going crazy?'

'The answer to both questions is no, Jean. As I was walking over here, I had a word with the Wilkinson sisters who were dressed in their finest. They told me they felt compelled to go to the cemetery but didn't know why. I also met with James Whittaker and he said the same thing. He was wearing a suit! Can you believe it?'

'I didn't even know he had one!'

A brief burst of laughter was replaced by nervousness, both women wondering what they might encounter on the other side of the wrought iron gates. There was only one way to find out.

Jean and Muriel linked arms for support and strolled down Stanhope Road. Turning left into Albemarle Street, they were astonished to see several other neighbours and friends, formally dressed and moving in the same direction. Some were carrying bunches of flowers whilst others walked empty-handed, but *everyone* looked confused as to why they had embarked on this particular action.

As they approached the cemetery, they met with more people coming from other parts of the town. Soon more than eighty had passed through the black gates, all slowly moving towards the graves of their loved ones. Len's resting place wasn't too far away from Jack's, so Muriel stayed with Jean for a while to give comfort and support. She noticed something odd and whispered to her friend.

'Have you realised that no-one's speaking?'

'Yes, Muriel, and there's something else. Apart from us, they're all standing still as statues. Why haven't *we* been affected like that?'

'It's probably because we're still talking, Jean. When I'm over at Len's graveside and you're on your own here, I'm sure we'll be as they are, waiting for something to happen. I'd best go there now but shout if you need me, alright?'

'I will. Thanks, Muriel.'

With that her friend walked away, leaving Jean nervously looking left and right at some of her fellow attendees. When

Muriel was in position, both women surrendered to the unspoken yet powerful need to remain motionless.

Nothing happened for several minutes, but suddenly all those gathered there looked down at the same time. Each person's eyes were focused on a central point in front of them, unblinking and resolute, their intense stares clearly an important factor in the afternoon's already odd proceedings. As one, however, the trance-like state was soon broken, and small movements in the ground started to occur.

Every stone sprang away to the grass edgings, followed by fallen leaves and small twigs, until the soil was completely clear of debris. A single shoot then emerged on each grave, initially paler than the surrounding grass blades, writhing and twisting until they stood a couple of inches tall. These new plants rapidly grew in stature, gaining colour as they did so, and it wasn't long before all were at eye-level. Every onlooker watched in amazement as pairs of leaves sprouted in front of them, followed by the immediate appearance of a single, tightly packed flower bud.

Jean threw a puzzled glance at Muriel, who simply offered a shrug and a hesitant smile. Curious mutterings amongst the crowd gradually rose to hubbub level, the communal noise only ceasing when a new sound became audible. It was a single, choral note that seemed to fill the air within moments. Initially pleasant, it rose in volume until several people covered their ears to shut it out. Finding this impossible, some started to scream against the vocal onslaught, but it suddenly cut out as quickly as it had arrived.

All were silent as each bloom slowly opened in unison, revealing a pair of eyes staring out for the first time. More petals folded back, and soon faces of recently departed or long deceased loved ones met the stares of their incredulous, open-mouthed relatives. With so many human flowers swaying in the

73

gentle afternoon breeze, the cemetery had become not just a resting place but a garden of the dead, however temporarily.

Nobody uttered a sound, so when the silence was shattered by the flower heads welcoming them as one, many people nearly fell over backwards with the shock. They recovered, ready to listen to the chorus of voices, who began by offering empathy and reassurance.

'We understand that you are all in a state of confusion, if not fear. We mean you no harm but ask that you hear our plea and, hopefully, act upon it.'

Without exception, the flowers twisted themselves and looked towards the newest graves before continuing to speak.

'Over there is the latest addition to our community, but no flower can bloom in that place.... yet. It belongs to a much-troubled little boy who was knocked down and killed by a hit and run driver. His name is Jake Stephens and he was only eight years old when he joined us last week. He told us he never knew his father and that his mother is seriously ill at home, so she couldn't come to his funeral. The only person who attended was Jake's grandmother, but she lives a long way from here so probably won't be able to visit Jake's grave again for a while.'

Every flower turned back to face its living audience member. After listening to this sad information delivered by such a strange chorus, the ensuing quiet took on a depth of meaning. Contemplations in the crowd were interrupted when the voices spoke again.

'Jake is the reason why we've asked you here this afternoon. He's hardly stopped crying since he arrived, and nothing seems to ease his distress. None of us can give Jake a hug, much as we'd like to, as we have no physical substance below ground. In fact, our time in these forms is limited and exhausting for us, so we must make our request without further delay.'

Cries of 'Tell us! Tell us!' and 'How can we help?' echoed around the cemetery.

'Thank you. Jake's needs are simple. Firstly, he needs to know that his mother is alright and wants someone to check on her regularly. He had become her young carer, balancing his schoolwork with cooking and cleaning at home. Her name is Carly and she lives at 34, Mill Street.'

Several people called out, saying that they lived nearby and would be more than happy to visit, every day if necessary.

'Wonderful. Thank you. Secondly, Jake would like flowers placed at the scene of his death. He often speaks of how Carly would send him to the local shop to buy a bunch for her. In fact, he was knocked down on the way home from buying some, and no-one on this side can begin to imagine his mother's growing panic while she waited for her boy to come home that afternoon.'

Amongst the sounds of sobbing, offers to comply with Jake's request came by the dozen.

'We felt sure you would want to help, knowing that there is a strong and lasting bond between all of us here. Oh, Jake has joined us. He's stopped crying and wants to thank you personally.'

The collective stopped speaking, and a single, tear-trembled voice took over.

'Hello. This is Jake. They try to help me here, I know they do, but I miss Mum so much and can't stop worrying about her. I'll need one of you to collect her tablets from the chemist every month. That's so important to me.'

The boy's faltering words ceased. A gentle whisper from the blooms, soft as the breeze, urged him to talk about the exact location of his death.

'I was knocked down on the pavement outside The Cottage Bakery. There's a lamp post nearby, so you could leave your flowers there, if you like.'

More whispering from the other side, and then....

'There is one other thing, but Jake has asked us to mention it as he is too embarrassed to do so.'

'Go on! Please! Anything!'

'Well, Jake has an old teddy bear called Mr. Jones. He's had him since he was four and he'd really love to see him again. I'm sure Carly wouldn't mind if one of you suggested that he could be left on Jake's grave, in memory of their time together. We won't have the strength to appear here again, but young Jake will be able to come through and say goodbye to Mr. Jones properly, even though he won't be able to hold him.'

Every member of the crowd now openly wept, eager to assuage the boy's pain as soon as possible. The voices from beyond offered reassurance, a warm smile of understanding on each flower's face.

'Jake says please don't cry for him anymore. He is so happy that you want to help and thanks you all for coming. He can rest easily now, knowing that Carly will be looked after in the way she deserves.'

A burst of spontaneous applause and cheering erupted, which was most unusual in such a setting. When all was quiet again, the ghostly chorus spoke for the final time.

'We thank you for helping our young friend but our energies here are fading fast. Soon we must return to our own world, however it has been wonderful to see you all, albeit for such a short time. Goodbye, dearest ones, and thank you again.'

With that, petals closed tightly around every face and the strange blooms decayed in seconds. Some of the visitors tried to gather up the blackened flowers but their intended keepsakes just crumbled away into dust. The stems, still with leaves attached, shrunk back into the soil, never to be seen again. A peculiar garden indeed, but with its purpose happily fulfilled.

As the crowd began to disperse, shaken but determined to carry out Jake's wishes, Muriel walked back to Jean. She was still crying.

'That poor boy. A life so needlessly cut short, and as for his mother....'

'I know, Jean, I know, but at least we've been given a chance to help both Jake *and* Carly.'

Muriel offered her friend a fresh tissue, and they started to walk towards the iron gates. Jean wiped away the trails of tears and considered the afternoon's events afresh.

'Let's not forget that we were able to see Len and Jack again, in a way. I never thought I'd be able to say *that*, Muriel, although I wish I could have heard Jack speaking on his own, just one last time.'

'I agree. I tried to shut out the other voices and concentrate on Len's, but it was impossible.'

'Never mind. Come back to mine for a coffee. I think we deserve a tot of brandy after what we've just been through!'

'I've got a better idea, Jean. Don't put it in the coffees. Instead we should raise a glass to Jake and his mother.'

'Perfect, Muriel!'

They linked arms and passed through the cemetery gates, happy in each other's support and companionship.

The lamp post outside The Cottage Bakery was festooned with bouquets of all sizes the next morning, and a selection of fresh flowers was continually maintained there. Although Carly found it hard to acknowledge the spot where Jake was killed, she took comfort in her visitors' photographs of the beautiful tributes, left nearby in his memory.

As for Mr. Jones, he was quietly placed on Jake's grave two days later. It was Pauline Hudson who left him there, and she also left her tears drying on the toy's yellow-furred chest. She couldn't bear to look back and hurried home, but in the late evening Pauline smiled to herself. She imagined the stones and leaves on Jake's grave scattering to the edges, after which he

would appear as a flower and look upon Mr. Jones for the very
last time.

THE RITUAL

Second prize. Second prize again. What's the point in bloody coming second? That doesn't mean anything, apart from telling you that you're not *quite* good enough. Oh, and then there's the pats on the back from your rivals and their sarcastic comments:

'Never mind, Morris. There's always next year, eh?'

'If you try that little bit harder, mate, you might win next time!'

Well, he had tried and tried and consistently missed out on the top prize. Morris had researched every aspect of rose cultivation and how to enter blooms in competitions, along with different composts, growth agents and pruning. All that effort edged with hope, with nothing to show but another disappointing drive home and a mocking piece of card with 'Second Prize' printed on it.

That was four years ago, however. Since then, Morris had consistently grabbed the top prize, wiping those thin smiles off his fellow competitors' faces. How he'd revelled in handing back their fake condolences, returned with a sneer:

'Bad luck, *mate,* but as they say, you can't win them all!'

Ah but he had, ever since the idea's seed was planted at the very table where he now sat.

On that occasion Morris had entered the kitchen, too burdened with the weight of rejection to eat anything and slumped down on the chair. He'd tossed that afternoon's offensive cardboard, along with one of his apparently second-rate roses, onto the table and just sat there staring at them. After a while, anger turned to activity and he ripped the card up four times. Still burning with frustration, Morris picked the rose up by the stem, and crushed it as hard as he could in his hand. The curved thorns cut deep into his flesh and he watched the blood drip onto the fragments of board. In that moment everything changed, and the notion of the ritual started to take root.

Morris won top prize at three shows during that summer. They say that revenge is sweet, and to Morris it was sweeter than the most fragrant rose ever grown. He was happy to feel the warm glow of success at last but wondered exactly *what* he had accessed in his garden shed, where the rite first took place. Good or evil? Angelic or demonic? No, it felt more like a pure connection with raw, unadulterated nature, merged seamlessly with his all-consuming desire to achieve absolute perfection.

He could see nothing wrong with what he was doing. After all no-one was getting hurt as a result (including himself as he'd kept his tetanus immunisation up to date), so why not continue year on year? Hadn't he waited long enough on the side lines, watching others basking in glory?

So, this is where we find Morris now, sitting in his kitchen on the eve of another show. He stands up and approaches the back door in the twilight.

The thick, navy blinds in the shed were pulled down two days earlier, so as not to arouse neighbourhood suspicion with a sudden, clandestine movement *this* evening. Morris walks to the bush from which he will select tomorrow's exhibition entries, and cuts two roses to use tonight. After unlocking the shed, he steps inside and bolts the door from within, placing the blooms on the floor.

He lights the red candle first (Rose *'Fragrant Cloud'*), and then the pink (*Rose 'Peace'*), leaving a space between them on the wooden shelf beneath the window. As the scents begin to circulate around the small space, Morris takes out the printed piece of card from a battered old filing cabinet and props it against an upturned terracotta flowerpot, set betwixt the candles (he stole the 'First Prize' notification from a judging table years ago when no-one was looking, correctly assuming that the panel would have spares).

To complete his preparations, Morris scatters compost all around, takes off his black polo shirt and kneels on the slatted floor. Tightly grabbing a rose in each fist and with eyes firmly shut, he violently rubs the thorn-laden stems against his bare chest. He manages to ignore the pain by beginning his chant:

'FIRST PRIZE IS MINE! FIRST PRIZE IS MINE!'

As Morris repeatedly states his self-affirmation, droplets of blood fall onto the compost-strewn surface, and it is at this point that the vision appears.

The first time it happened, Morris was completely taken by surprise, but he soon learnt to accept it as an integral part of the ceremony.

He is standing beneath a brilliant blue sky, dressed in his crisp white shirt, olive-green chinos and sand-brown cotton jacket. This is the outfit he wore when he won his first top accolade and has done so at every competitive event since.

Morris's eyes are wide open here, and his vision is filled with rose bed after rose bed, disappearing into the far distance. All colours and varieties are spread before him, from floribunda to hybrid tea, from shrub to miniature. Even climbing roses are represented, forming a natural border and framing the picturesque scene. He drinks in both the vibrant and pastel shades, and breathes deeply through his nose, experiencing as many different scents as possible in his own perfect rose garden. As with previous visits to this alternate reality, the perfumes intensify and overwhelm him, and he collapses onto the floorboards in a state of sensory intoxication.

'First prize is mine. First prize is mine.'

Morris continues to mumble the phrase until he falls asleep amongst the rose petals, blooded stems and compost, as he has done several times before.

Morris will awaken two hours later, stand up and blow out the rose-scented candles. He will put his polo shirt back on, satisfied that the wounds are already in the process of healing. He will smile to himself as he walks back down the garden, acknowledging that everything *is* all moonlight and roses. In the morning, he will iron his white shirt and press his olive-green chinos. With blooms selected, cut and carefully packed for the journey, he will slip on his sand-brown cotton jacket and set off for the competition venue.

Maybe a rose by any other name *would* smell as sweet. As far as Morris is concerned, however, the nameless, indefinable bond between himself and nature will be all that matters, when he finds a 'First Prize' card placed next to his display on yet another victorious afternoon.

BRAIN FOOD

How had it come to this sorry state of affairs? Reg looked across the kitchen table at Stella and considered the last word in the question, even though he had always been a faithful and dutiful husband.

Their marriage of 38 years appeared to outsiders to be one of domestic bliss, unshakable and secure, but when the couple were alone together the situation was far from happy. Increasingly, Stella had belittled her beleaguered husband, criticising everything about him. The way he slurped his soup, the way he cleared his throat, the way he.... the way his.... everything! Even when Reg tried to change or adapt his behaviour in order to please her, Stella would find fresh annoyances to hurl at him, thus maintaining the constant barrage of nit-picking remarks.

There was one quibble to which she kept returning, namely his bald pate. Reg had started to lose his hair in his early twenties, following the male pattern baldness experienced by his father around the same age. It never particularly bothered him, and he endured the usual tired old jokes from friends and colleagues, such as:

'Reg, when you go to the barbers for a haircut, do they ask you which one?' or 'Does your barber have to send out a search party?'

Such hilarity and *so* original. No, what surprised him much more were the reactions of people when they passed by in the street. On countless occasions men or women would raise a hand to their heads, as if checking that their hair was still in place, or consciously hoping to make Reg feel inadequate in his bald state (if the latter, they were wasting their time).

During their courtship and early years of marriage, Stella barely mentioned her partner's alopecia. Reg, quite reasonably, assumed that it wasn't an issue for her either, but then needling little questions started to creep into their conversations, like:

'I wonder how much hair transplants cost?'

Stella began insisting that Reg wore a hat when they went out together, as if she was embarrassed to be seen with him. He complied with her request for a few months but then refused, taking pleasure in his little piece of rebellion.

The frequency of Stella's sideswipes had dramatically increased lately, to the extent that Reg started to count the barbed remarks spewing from her lips. He calculated the average to be five per hour during the day, four per hour in the evening period and three during the night. These last comments, invariably as a reaction to Reg's snoring, were always accompanied by a sharp dig in the ribs.

Every needling insult, every groundless accusation, had gradually coalesced into a pure hatred – yes, that was the right word – *hatred* for his wife. Reg's mood had darkened considerably recently, and he now felt like some caged animal, taunted and poked with a stick from outside the bars by someone for whom he used to feel genuine love. Not anymore.

Stella was a terrible cook, but it never mattered because Reg was a dab hand in the kitchen. Until recently, he had always tried to provide interesting vegetarian food for them both, knowing about her preference from the start of their relationship. Stella's choice was not due to any environmental or ethical standpoint, rather that she just couldn't bear the smell of meat being roasted, stewed or especially fried. Reg, on the other hand, missed the sizzle of sausages or the crackle of bacon and longed for such delights to pass his lips again. He took pleasure in imagining the still-warm grease trickling into his grey-white goatee beard, his facial hair another source of intense irritation for Stella. Since growing it, she had shunned any closeness on his part in order to avoid 'that scratchy bloody thing' against her face. Clearly, his plan had worked.

Everything came to a head, so to speak, one teatime in June after Stella was served baked beans on toast. She looked down at her plate and then up at Reg. He felt her scornful eyes burn into him and waited for the vitriol to spew from her thin lips.

'Is this all you can be bothered to cook then, dearest husband?'

How he despised her when she used that fake term of endearment. He fired back a sarcastic question.

'It looks that way, doesn't it?'

'How *dare* you speak to me like that!'

Stella pushed the plate violently across the kitchen table and waited for an apology. None came so she stood up, slapped his face hard then stormed out of the back door and into the garden. Reg stood at the kitchen window with his cheek smarting and watched as his wife in name only kicked over a few empty flowerpots. She briefly turned and looked daggers at him, before running towards the back fence where she stood stock still with her fists clenched in rage.

Reg, ever dutiful but unappreciated, wearily scraped the warm food into the bin. Stella was right. He just couldn't be bothered to prepare anything but the simplest meals anymore, the days of appetising soups or enticing curries long gone.

Something prickled on his head as he looked back at the contemptible figure in the garden. Reg yielded to an urgent need to scratch at several points, but the itch just wouldn't go away, in fact it intensified until he could hardly bear it. He rushed upstairs to the bathroom and stared into the mirror, amazed to find six wiry growths protruding from his scalp.

Reg shaved his head every day to ensure Stella was in a constant state of annoyance, so how could these white, wispy strands have been missed? He grabbed his trusty razor and tried to remove them, but they stubbornly remained in position.

'Damn it! I meant to get some new blades last week, but that dreadful woman kept going on and on about what *she* wanted at the shops and I clean forgot. I HATE HER SO MUCH!'

New blades wouldn't have made any difference. Reg had grasped the sink's edge during his outburst but loosened his grip when he looked at the hairs again. They had grown longer and thicker, seemingly fed by his antipathy towards Stella. Seeking to test this strange notion Reg spat her name out several times, laced with derision, and watched as the stems became yet more robust. Taking the experiment further, he gave voice to something that had been building for some time:

'I WANT TO KILL HER! I WANT TO KILL HER!'

The plants frantically twisted and writhed upwards, turning from white to vivid green and producing heart-shaped leaves as they grew. It was such a surreal sight, yet it all made sense to Reg. These botanical growths were clearly a manifestation of his loathing towards Stella, a hate-seeded garden sprouting directly from his brain.

'Where are you, dearest husband? Are you hiding upstairs? You're pathetic, you really are!'

Suddenly panicked, Reg knew that he couldn't let Stella see his new appearance. At best she would burst into mocking laughter, at worst she would come at him with a pair of scissors, not caring if she injured him in the pruning process. He rushed down the stairs, grabbed his knitted bobble hat from the wall-mounted coat rack and hurriedly put it over the flourishing plant life. The increasingly ill-matched couple met in the hallway.

'Oh, so this is the latest thing to annoy me with, is it? Well you can keep that on forever for all I care. You always were an oddball, dearest husband, but this is ridiculous! I wish I'd never met you, you weirdo!'

Stella pushed past him and stomped upstairs. The bedroom door slammed shut, and Reg waited a few minutes until he was sure that she was taking a rest. He went through to the lounge with a view to having forty winks himself, but he closed the door first so that he would have fair warning if Stella entered the room. He imagined her sneaking in, pulling the hat down hard over his face and holding it there while he struggled to breathe, laughing as she did so.

Reg sat down and soon drifted into a pleasant slumber. Gradually he became aware of a strange tickling sensation underneath his scalp, during which an image came into sharp focus. He was sitting at the kitchen table with Stella, having just set a plate of vivid green salad leaves before her. She was smiling at him, a warmth he hadn't encountered for many a month. Everything appeared to be in slow motion, as if Reg was being encouraged to take in every detail, and then he realised. The leaves on Stella's plate were heart-shaped, just like those concealed under his bobble hat. He forced himself to watch as his wife put a forkful of salad into her mouth, and then the whole vision disappeared, replaced by a pure white 'screen'.

Reg awoke with a start and sat bolt upright, trying to find an explanation for such odd imagery. It wasn't so much that he suddenly understood what he'd just dreamt, more that his brain *made* him accept the scene for what it was, a manifestation of pure malice.

He took off his woollen hat and ran the fingers of his left hand through the leafy growths, the connection strengthening further.

Reg knew exactly what had to be done and calmly returned to the bathroom.

'Tea's ready!'

Stella opened the bedroom door, grumbling about having been woken up. With a heavy tread she came downstairs, dishevelled and half asleep.

'There's no need to shout! It'd better not be bloody baked beans again, dearest husband. I can't take any more!'

Reg knew *that* feeling only too well. He forced a smile when Stella entered the kitchen.

'At last you've seen sense and taken that stupid hat off! Let's face it. You're just a tired old slap head, so there's no point in trying to hide the fact. Now, where's my tea?'

She sat down at the table, feigning impatience and sighing loudly. Her quiet husband looked at the 'special' salad for a few moments, before lifting the plate from the marbled work surface and placing it in front of Stella. He sat opposite her and waited for the inevitable abuse to begin.

'A *salad*? Is that the best you can do, dearest husband? It's not even a proper one! It's just a load of funny shaped leaves! Aren't *you* having any?'

'I'm.... not really that hungry. Besides it's for *you*, so tuck in.'

What was wrong with him? He was never this assertive and he certainly hadn't provided any unusual or interesting food for a long time. Stella eyed him suspiciously as he sat down. She lifted her fork, but then paused to ask a question.

'Where did you buy this stuff? I've never seen anything like it when *I've* been in the supermarket!'

Reg, still smiling, carefully chose and weighed his words before answering.

'Oh.... they're home grown and completely natural. Please, enjoy!'

A cynical sneer spread across Stella's face. Reg eagerly watched as she pushed the tines into the green mass, then moved both cutlery and leaves towards her lips. Even though he had snipped the stems flush to his scalp, he felt the roots tingle underneath his skin in anticipation.

A reaction took place as soon as the forkful entered her open mouth. The leaves lost their shape, amassing into a vivid green bolus that forced its way down her throat, swelling as it moved. Stella, unable to speak, stretched out her arms but the desperate gesture elicited no response from Reg. He just sat motionless with his arms folded, watching her as she gurgled through her last few moments.

The weight of the green mass tipped Stella's head forwards, and soon the leaves had returned to their former shapes and dropped back onto the plate. Through them, Reg had achieved what he'd secretly longed for over many months. He watched as they shrivelled to nothing and felt the roots in his head crumble away at the same time. With their purpose achieved they had no need to exist and, best of all, they left no trace inside Stella's now lifeless body.

'I'll contact the doctor in a couple of hours, dearest wife. I just want to savour this moment.'

Twenty minutes after murdering Stella, Reg calmly walked to the small supermarket in the next street and bought a pack of eight sausages. No-one saw or spoke to him, although he almost wished they had as any encounter would have provided an alibi. No matter. The death looked natural enough.

Back at home and whistling, Reg took a large frying pan from the cupboard and poured in a little oil, before snipping the skin between each sausage. Placing them on a medium heat, Reg's heart filled with joy. He listened to the familiar but much-missed sizzle as it grew louder and salivated at the delicious thought of tasting meat again.

IN MINIATURE

'But I swear she was right here next to me! She can't have just vanished!'

Tracy Hughes took a fresh tissue from the small packet and wiped away her latest tears. Mick put his arm around his distraught wife's shoulder, but she pushed him away. Her only focus was the whereabouts of her daughter and what might have happened. The young police officer attempted to offer reassurance, employing a quiet tone of voice she had learnt during training.

'Poppy can't have gone far, Mrs. Hughes. I'm sure she's still in the village and that my colleagues will soon find her.'

'But she's only six! What if someone's taken my little Poppy away? I mean, you hear about these things on the news and how it only takes a moment for…. for….'

The thought of the little girl being snatched away stopped Tracy in her tracks and she fell silent, numbed by the disturbing imagery crowding her mind. Mick, feeling somewhat helpless in the situation, decided on a course of action.

'Look, love. You stay here with Constable Jarvis and I'll go and check at the ticket office. You never know - they might have news for us. If not, I could ask some of the other visitors if they've seen a little girl with blonde hair walking around looking lost. Sounds like a plan?'

Tracy nodded, accepting his reasoning.

'Do you want to go with Dad, Owen?'

The sullen ten-year-old shook his head and stared down at his scuffed trainers. He saw Poppy's disappearance as just another example of her getting all the attention and found it hard to care where she'd gone. Mick kissed his wife on the cheek and set off for the only full-sized building nearby, fervently hoping that this would soon all be over.

Like Owen, Mick hadn't really wanted to come here for the family holiday. His son had protested in no uncertain terms that there would be nothing to do on the coast, voicing his preference on several occasions that he'd rather go to a large theme park somewhere. Although not wanting to take sides in the discussions, Mick had secretly longed for something similar. He often imagined himself gripping onto the rails during a blood-curdling rollercoaster ride and screaming at the top of his voice as the train repeatedly hurtled downwards then climbed again. Each time the subject came up, however, he accepted Tracy's viewpoint, namely that Poppy was too young for such a vacation and that a quieter holiday would be much more suitable.

Which is how they had come to spend a week here, a medium-sized town on the south coast, slightly frayed around the edges and long past its glory days. Everything felt tired, from the décor in their nondescript hotel to the not very amusing amusement arcades. These were staffed by people who would clearly rather be somewhere else, any desire to escape leached away over time like pebbles gradually worn down by the tide.

The only member of the family who was really enjoying the holiday was little Poppy (*where is she?*). Owen had grudgingly admitted to having fun on the dodgems on Monday, and his Dad had loved them as it took him back to his *own* childhood, but it was his sister who thought she'd found somewhere truly special.

It was on Tuesday afternoon that they first visited the model village. Owen displayed his boredom with fake yawns throughout, but Poppy (*has somebody taken her?*) skipped merrily along the winding path, stopping every so often to gaze at the miniature people at her feet. She loved the sensation of being taller than all the houses, imagining that this must be how it feels to be a giant. The enthralled child saw figures in all sorts of situations. Some were waiting on train platforms, whilst others walked through the churchyard. There was even a well-attended folk festival complete with musicians, but it was those looking after the beautiful gardens who really appealed to her.

Although Poppy (*where's she gone?*) couldn't name it as a six-year-old, it was this specific difference in scale that fascinated her. The diminutive gardeners tended their small lawns and vegetable patches in the shade of what to them were enormous shrubs, with massive trees in the background.

When her parents informed her that it was time to leave (a moment that Owen felt was long overdue), Poppy made it crystal clear that she didn't agree. She burst into tears and stamped her feet, causing several other visitors to stare in her direction. Eventually Mick had to carry her away from the scene, and she only stopped protesting when an ice cream was offered to pacify her (*she could have* twenty *ice creams if she'd only come back to us now*).

'MODEL VILLAGE! MODEL VILLAGE!'

'But we went there yesterday, Poppy. Aren't there are other places you'd like to visit?'

'MODEL VILLAGE! MODEL VILLAGE!'

'There's a zoo not far from here. Wouldn't you like to see some lovely animals?'

'NO, DADDY! MODEL VILLAGE!'

'Alright then, Poppy. I suppose we can go there again if you like.'

'That's so unfair, Dad! Why does she always get what she wants? You haven't even *asked* me!'

Owen ran into the hotel bedroom he was sharing with his sister and slammed the door. After lengthy negotiations involving computer game inducements, he emerged an hour later and mumbled an apology.

Poppy ran straight to her favourite miniature gardens in the model village (*why can't we find her?*) and stood staring down at the men and women looking after lawns, flowers and vegetables. Her parents noticed that she was not only smiling at the miniature people but also quietly talking to them. They weren't unduly concerned by this behaviour, dismissing it as merely a little girl's fantasy. Owen, on the other hand, said it proved that his sister was 'completely crazy', a viewpoint he'd often expressed before. The truth was very different, however, for Poppy was whispering to the gardening figures that she would love to join them. She repeated her wish many times until it became an imploring chant (*how I long to hear her voice again*), eyes fixed firmly on the people near her powder blue shoes.

She suddenly broke free and ran to her family, smiling broadly as her brother scowled.

'Look! She's finished. Can we go now, *please*?'

Owen had had enough of this place. He wanted to kick every house over and trample them into nothing. He wanted to stamp on as many of the little people as possible, imagining the pleasure brought about by their screams for mercy as his trainers came down from above.

He could hardly believe it when his parents capitulated yet again the next day, yielding to his infuriating sister's demands. Owen trudged along behind them in silence, kicking at lamp posts along the way. Dressed only in black, Owen sneered at Poppy's bright yellow summer dress with its bright blue sash around her waist.

The family passed through the turnstiles, and the excited little girl hurried to the scaled-down gardens. She immediately started to whisper again, if anything more fervently than yesterday. Mum, Dad and Owen caught up with Poppy and stood nearby. They must all have briefly looked away at the same time (*oh, if only we hadn't*), because….

'I swear that's the last time we saw her! Do you think I'm lying, Constable Jarvis? Well, do you?'

Mick had rushed back to his wife's side after visiting the ticket office. Nobody had described seeing a small child wandering around on her own, but he was told that Poppy's disappearance had been announced several times over the tannoy system after one of the police officers first reported it. Mick realised that he must have been too distressed to hear the message being broadcast and thanked the staff member for her assistance. As promised, he'd also asked a few visitors if they had seen Poppy, but their blank expressions and shrugged shoulders only added to his feelings of helplessness.

Constable Jarvis tried to calm the already heated situation.

'Please, Mr. Hughes! No-one's accusing you of anything but, as I say, I do need to ask you both to go through your accounts again, just in case you've missed out any small details that might prove important. I'll ask your son to do the same later.'

For the second time, Mick and Tracy recounted the events of the afternoon. Mick just managed to keep his temper in check (*I've told you all I know! Now fucking find my daughter!*). Tracy fought back a fresh wave of tears, all the while wanting to scream a desperate mother's plea out loud (*Please, PLEASE find my little Poppy!*).

Everyone seemed to have forgotten about Owen who was standing a few feet away, but then he'd become used to that. Since Poppy was born, all the attention previously lavished on him had simply ebbed way, causing resentment to slowly build in his young heart.

Distractedly, Owen glanced down at the miniature flower beds and lawns, and something there caught his eye.

Among the static figures was one in a bright yellow dress with a blue waistband. Owen squatted down to get a closer look and noticed that this little gardener had blonde hair. She was holding a basket of freshly picked flowers and was fixed in a mid-walking position.

He smirked and stood up, ready to seize the opportunity of becoming the favoured child, indeed the only child, once more. Owen glanced at his distraught parents as they grappled with their deep distress, but he felt only a delightful calm. With his left trainer, he discreetly nudged his static sister away from the gardens and into the shadow cast by a bush nearby.

Owen moved towards his frantic parents. Dad was shouting at the policewoman with his arms flailing, and Mum had started to tremble uncontrollably. He suppressed the need to burst out laughing and placed his arms around their shoulders in a show of empathy and support.

OPEN (WARFARE) DAY

'No, Gerald! Not those ones! Are you mad?'

'What do you mean, Marjorie?'

'I won't run the risk of having my best porcelain chipped or broken, so pass me the service from the lower cupboard. We have no idea who might turn up this afternoon!'

Surely that was the whole point of having an open day, Gerald thought, but decided against voicing his opinion. The morning had been stressful enough without adding another layer of argument to the mix. Marjorie had been issuing orders to her husband since breakfast, ticking off each item on a long list after they had been fulfilled. As he placed the best crockery back in the cupboard, Gerald wished he hadn't 'agreed' to this whole charade in the first place.

Gerald and Marjorie had lived at No. 1, The Crescent for just under four years, an exclusive development on the outskirts of town. The size of the garden had been the main factor in deciding to purchase the property, and the couple enjoyed shaping, planning and planting the large space three weeks after moving in. The lawn was extensive, however, and Gerald often wished he could just pave over the whole damn lot, this thought at its height each time he was halfway through mowing in the summer heat.

The subject of today's event first arose during breakfast on a Sunday morning back in May. Marjorie, without any discussion or forewarning, announced that they would be holding an Open Day in July. Gerald slowly lowered his newspaper and gave his wife a quizzical look over his half-moon glasses (he knew she hated him reading the paper at the table, which was precisely why he did it).

'Whatever gave you that idea? Might I suppose that one of the Bridge Club ladies is having one soon as well?'

Damn him. He always seemed to know when a plan or ploy was afoot, especially when it involved getting one up on Marjorie's rivals in one of her social groups. She smiled nonchalantly, trying to affect an air of innocence.

'I'm sure I don't know what you mean. It just so happens that Pamela is hosting one in early August, but that has no bearing on my decision. I just thought it would be rather nice, that's all.'

Gerald didn't believe a word of it and raised his newspaper with a derogatory sniff. He knew that Marjorie would loathe every minute of giving 'the public', as she often dismissively called them, access to their well-tended private space, and that her forced, welcoming smile to all and sundry would be offered through clenched teeth. Marjorie took Gerald's silence to mean that he agreed with the Open Day. She started to sketch out ideas for the event that very morning, and now the big day had arrived.

Marjorie enjoyed arranging the assortment of cakes and fancies (home-made, of course) on doily-dressed serving plates. She went through the same procedure with her symmetrical sandwiches, but earlier the decision as to their fillings had become a major issue, until Gerald couldn't take any more.

'They can have cream cheese or tuna and cucumber and bloody like it, Marjorie!'

'Please watch your tongue! I will NOT have you swearing in front of our guests this afternoon! Now go and check everything looks perfect outside, if that's not too much trouble.'

Happy to be temporarily out of the firing line, Gerald sloped off into the garden for yet another inspection, ready to focus on the task in hand.

Gerald had to admit that everything did indeed look perfect and he was secretly proud of the lawn. It was immaculate and beautifully striped (but does she ever appreciate how long it takes, or how much I hate doing it?), with all the edges precisely trimmed, as if by nail scissors. He walked along the border on

97

the right-hand side, drinking in the wonderful colour palette in the sunshine. Yellow gazanias, striped with dark red, took pride of place in the foreground, with hardy geraniums close by, subtle in their shade of pink. Further back stood purple alliums, looking like floral versions of lollipops on their thin stems. Red hot pokers sat behind these, dramatic in their tones of yellow and orange, but it was the blooms at the back of this planting arrangement that really grabbed Gerald's attention. For there, in shades of blue, mauve and pink was an impressive display of delphiniums, head and shoulders above everything else. He stepped back to the middle of the lawn to enjoy the overall effect, before walking to the end of the garden.

Gerald moved past the sizeable shed which was situated between two large lilac trees. He made a mental note that he must get a new padlock and fitting, something he'd meant to do since he damaged it a few weeks ago. Marjorie had annoyed him so much one evening that he'd stormed down the garden and high-kicked the door extremely hard, irreparably damaging the original fixture.

Strolling back down the other side, Gerald paused to look at the bright purples and scarlets of three well-established fuchsias, then walked on to a large white hydrangea. The shrub had never looked so good, and Gerald became entangled in the happy memory of planting it there, back before his marriage descended into acrimony and discord.

At least he had his Chloe. She made everything seem simple, joyful even, and he couldn't imagine life without her. Of course, he was unable to see Chloe as often as he would like. They managed to be together once a week, because Marjorie's Bridge Club took place on Tuesday afternoons a few streets away. She hosted a coffee morning every Friday, and Gerald loathed these dull events. Not because they were so boring, full of small talk and cupcakes, but because he couldn't visit Chloe. On such occasions, he resented his wife more than ever and longed to be somewhere else.

Chloe's real name was Graham Turner. He owned a successful car rental business and lived in the centre of town at No. 57, Carlisle Street. Gerald had his own key to the small terraced house and would discreetly let himself in, checking before entering that the coast was clear. In fact, discretion was at the heart of their arrangement. There was nothing sordid or sexual about it. Chloe would be waiting for her visitor in the bedroom, dressed elegantly in a silk kimono. She had several, but Gerald especially liked the one with scarlet flowers on a pale blue background, so it was this garment that she usually wore.

They would just sit on the bed together, holding hands and enjoying the stillness of the room. Gerald had no desire to dress in a similar fashion or wear make-up, and Graham just appreciated being appreciated for his other persona. After an hour, Gerald always stood up, smiled at his private companion and quietly left No. 57. As soon as the front door closed, Chloe would move across to her dressing table and sit staring at the mirror for a few moments. She would then gradually become Graham again, ready to return to the office to face the inevitable tide of emails and enquiries. Mr. Turner always felt revitalised somehow and knew that his confidante shared this sense of completeness, even though they never discussed it, or anything, for that matter.

Gerald walked to the rose bed, wryly savouring the irony that life for him was anything *but* a bed of roses, apart from Chloe, of course. How could he wait until Tuesday afternoon? To ease his pain, he touched the petals of a pale pink bloom, happy that at least he'd kept *this* secret from Marjorie. Many months ago, when they were deciding on their choice of roses, Gerald had oh-so-innocently suggested a shrub variety called 'Chloe'. He

99

passed the catalogue to his wife and was inwardly overjoyed when she agreed with his suggestion. Standing there now, Gerald realised that it would be impossible to count the times he'd simply gazed at these flowers and whispered her name. Yes, he'd taken quite a risk in answering Graham's advertisement online, especially when he discovered that the advertiser lived locally, but it had worked out well for them both. Besides, it seemed to Gerald that Mr. Turner (alias Chloe) had much more to lose. He was well known as a businessman in the town, whereas Gerald had been retired from the bank for nearly a decade.

A short series of sharp raps on the kitchen window forced Gerald out of his contemplation, and he reluctantly took his hand away from his acquaintance's floral namesake. As he walked towards the house, he noticed how Marjorie's face looked sour and aggressive through the glass, and he wearily wondered what she was going to complain about next.

'Don't just lurk in the garden, Gerald! A car has just arrived so go and open the side gate for our visitors. I had a quick peek through the nets in the living room as they were getting out, and they look rather unsavoury to me.'

'Unsavoury, Marjorie? You haven't even met them yet! You really have become an incredible snob since we moved here.'

'What an outrageous thing to say! I just have certain standards to maintain, that's all. Now go and greet them while I finish off the refreshments.'

Gerald did as he was told as usual. He opened the gate and was met by a young family of four.

'Hi there, I'm Dom. This is my lovely wife, Bernie, and these are our kids, Fern and Laurel.'

'Pleased to meet you, I'm Gerald. Do come through. Marjorie, my wife, is rather busy in the kitchen but she'll join us shortly. Are you from around here?'

'No, we live about ten miles away. We were just out for a drive and saw the sign in your front garden, so thought we'd pop in and have a look.'

'Oh good. That lettering took ages so I'm glad it caught your attention. Do you enjoy gardening yourselves?'

'We do, but nothing on this scale. The girls have got their own veg patch which keeps them out of mischief, for a while at least!'

The adults laughed and the ten-year old twins' faces flushed with embarrassment, but then Gerald heard an intermittent hissing sound coming from the kitchen.

'Excuse me for a moment.'

'Come in and close the door!'

'Whatever's the matter, Marjorie?'

'I never expected anyone with children to visit us! They're bound to run amok, trampling everything and making lots of noise!'

'Fern and Laurel are actually very well behaved.'

'FERN AND LAUREL? How ridiculous!'

'Well I think they're really nice names, and Dom and Bernie are trying to get their daughters interested in gardening, which is a good thing.'

'Dom? Bernie? You know how much I abhor abbreviated names! I simply can't come and meet them, so you'll have to deal with this.'

'You've completely misjudged them and you're being totally unreasonable.'

'It's no good! I'm going upstairs for a lie down.'

'Fine! Leave it all to me!'

Two more cars arrived as Marjorie headed for the stairs, leaving Gerald to walk to the side gate to greet the newcomers. John and Tony had just bought their first property together and were looking for planting ideas. Tim and Lara lived a few streets away and were curious to see one of the gardens in The Crescent. Like Dom and Bernie, both couples had seen the sign as they drove past.

Gerald, despite his earlier misgivings about the Open Day, found that he was soon thoroughly enjoying himself. He ferried plates of sandwiches and cakes from the kitchen to his guests and made copious cups of tea and coffee. He chatted and laughed with his visitors and occasionally offered gardening tips. Gerald saw them as 'his', having been abandoned by Marjorie to cope with everything, but he didn't mind.

Every so often, Gerald would glance in the direction of 'that rose' and think of his Chloe, sitting on the bed beside him at No. 57. He knew that Marjorie was watching him from the bedroom window, because he'd noticed the net curtains moving more than once, out of the corner of his eye.

At one point, there were well over a dozen people looking round the garden. Some had younger children than Fern and Laurel, and it was these juveniles who proved to be the final straw for Marjorie.

She tore down the nets, flung the windows wide and let out a hate-filled scream. Gerald's guests stopped talking and eating, and all the kids froze in mid-play. Everyone looked up, wondering what would happen next, and then a stream of invective filled the air.

'This isn't what I was hoping for at all! I wanted to have well-dressed, attractive visitors, and it's clear that none of you have made any effort in that department. I was looking forward to greeting guests with bearing and a certain je ne sais quoi, and none of you possess those qualities. I'm sorely disappointed with how this afternoon has turned out, and I'm particularly upset that some of you decided to bring your revolting children with you. I won't thank you for coming because, quite frankly, I rather wish you hadn't, and now I think it best if you all just leave. My husband will escort everyone off the premises. Do as I ask, Gerald, and as soon as possible. Gerald? GERALD!'

The only sounds in the garden after the tirade of abuse were of several children crying, and of parents trying to comfort them. Gerald looked around at his visitors, every one of whom had made his afternoon a delight. He slowly raised his eyes to the bedroom window, where Marjorie was shooing the small crowd towards the side gate with rapid hand gestures. Then the worm turned.

'NO, Marjorie! They're good people, something you would have discovered for yourself if you hadn't decided to stay up there in your tower all afternoon! As for your nasty little speech just now, what gives you the right to judge ANYBODY? Are *you* perfect? Well, I certainly don't think so! In fact, you've made me realise how much you've changed since we moved here. You were always a bit snooty, but you're much worse than that now, obsessed with your ridiculous etiquette and social standing!'

'Gerald! Come up here this instant! I will NOT be spoken to in this manner!'

'Oh, really, Your Highness? Well I think you might be about to face a rebellion!'

Gerald turned away in order to address his audience on the lawn.

'You all heard what Madam thinks of you, your appearance and your children, all of whom have been much better behaved than she has today, so a question arises. Are we going to put up with this?'

Everyone stood in awkward silence, their English reserve causing nervousness and an unwillingness to participate. Gerald noticed their reticence, so decided to muster his troops.

'WELL ARE WE?'

A defiant cry of 'NO!' rang out which reached the other residents in The Crescent, all of whom had listened to Marjorie's outburst whilst ostensibly tending *their* gardens with smirks on their faces.

'Come on then! Follow me!'

Gerald shot his wife a look of utter contempt and turned towards the shed. When he reached the door, he issued another high kick, this time dislodging the bolt and padlock completely. The revolt's leader then handed out spades, forks, rakes and pairs of shears to the adults, and trowels to the children.

'Here, take these! I'm sure you know what to do.'

With all decorum abandoned, the parents ran around the garden screaming like banshees, encouraging their offspring to whoop and shout. All brandished their tools of insurgency with pride and selected a spot along the large border. Then, on Gerald's command, everyone set about destroying each plant with vigour and aggression.

Marjorie was forced to watch helplessly as the scene of horticultural carnage spread to the other side of the garden. The hydrangea was soon reduced to little more than white blossom and broken stems, and every rose bush was dug up and trampled down. Gerald's heart sank when he saw Chloe laying uprooted on the soil but knew that to lose 'his' rose was a sacrifice that had to be borne bravely. Because of this loss his rage intensified, and he considered a final humiliation, one that would be particularly upsetting for Marjorie and extremely pleasing to him.

Gerald ran behind the shed and took the covers off his top-of-the-range lawnmower. After adjusting the blade to cut a little deeper than usual, he shouted to his loyal followers to step back onto the now-ruined flower beds. He emerged onto the grass with the machine running and proceeded to cut deliberate diagonals and random curves into the immaculate stripes, laughing like a maniac as he did so. The small crowd put down their implements and cheered him on, but Marjorie clasped her hands to her face in horror. Part of her wanted to run downstairs and plead with them to stop, but she knew that any such action would be foolish to say the least. Some of those tools were sharp.

Gerald switched off the lawnmower then whispered something to one of the children, who then ran off and told the others. He fetched a couple of large saws from the shed and handed them to the assembled grown-ups.

'Right then! I'm off. Take these and cut down the lilacs for me, and let your lovely children do their worst. Then, if you don't mind, leave by the side gate and ignore my wife's screams as you go. Thank you so much for all your help this afternoon. It's been such a pleasure having every one of you here, but now there's somewhere else I need to be.'

All the adults shook Gerald's hand or patted him on the back. Before leaving the scene of devastation, he glanced up at Marjorie for the last time, with plans for a new life already in embryonic form. He would rent a small flat in town, somewhere not too far from Carlisle Street. Released from the restrictions of Marjorie's social schedule, he would be able to visit Chloe more often. He reached the side gate with that tender thought playing on his mind and turned to watch the final stages of the afternoon's campaign. The felling of the trees was already underway, and the children were merrily gouging out lumps of lawn, tossing the clods aside with glee.

Gerald pulled the gate to and opened the car door. He knew that Mr. Turner would be in his office for just over an hour, but no matter. He would park on Carlisle Street and wait for Graham to enter No. 57, before discreetly knocking at the door a few minutes later. Gerald felt sure that once over the initial shock of an unscheduled visit he would be welcomed inside. He'd probably be asked to wait in the lounge until Chloe called for him to go through to the bedroom.

Gerald closed the car door and started the engine, happy to be leaving. He smiled at the sound of Marjorie's continuing screams in the background and revelled in the thought of seeing that pale blue kimono with the scarlet flowers again.

BROODBIO:01
(hope is all we have)

What follows is a selection of entries taken from a highly personal account, created by an individual with the burden of an uncertain future on his young shoulders. Also included are occasional interjections from some of his increasingly concerned guardians.

22/01/2092

I've finally agreed to start my journal today. It's my 15th birthday. Well, it's all our birthdays, in fact. There was a huge celebration in The Great Hall this evening. It was very special for us because we've never been allowed in there before. Every Elder was present, along with most of the top scientists from the laboratory. Several members of The Party came to meet us, although they didn't talk to us for long. They seemed more interested in studying data and forecasts, and I noticed that they appeared rather nervous every time we looked at them.

I haven't been that bothered about this journal to be honest, but Elder Karim has been going on and on about how important it is for my cohort to chronicle our lives from this point, and how one day we'll understand how special we are. It's not as if we haven't been closely monitored over our first fifteen years. Far from it.

Every morning, afternoon and evening we go through a series of tests, including the taking of fluid samples and a range of physical exercises, and our diet is strictly controlled. We're not allowed to eat the ordinary green matter everyone else enjoys. Instead we're given highly concentrated organic material. Something about boosting our refined immune systems, or so Elder Sienna says.

I feel it's important to include details of my schooldays here, seeing as this is my first entry. I am one of a group of forty, divided into two equal sets for lessons. Our 'school' is part of a large country estate, set many kilometres away from any town or city. We've lived here all our lives and are looked after well, although sometimes I wonder what ordinary life is like. Some of us discuss this in our free time, even though we know everything we say or do is being observed.

Elder Karim told me I should be completely honest in what I say in my journal. So be it. Personally, I can't wait to experience a new life away from here. I know we've been part of an experiment from Day One, and I know we're seen as 'the future', but what if it goes wrong? What if this is all just a false hope, and we're only delaying the end?

I'm not the only one with doubts and questions, especially during Biohistory lessons. Of course, it's terrible that humans can't conceive any more due to the sperm count dropping to zero resulting in a population decline worldwide, but is it *my* fault that decades of concern over pollution were consistently ignored? We were taught that a large cloning programme took place twenty years ago, but when I've asked why this didn't prove to be the answer, I'm just told that major problems arose, and that future research has been banned.

Don't get me wrong. Most of the time I *do* feel honoured to be part of a possible solution to all this, but deep down I resent being someone, *something* that came out of a laboratory. I'm getting tired now so I'm going to end this entry here.

I close with a message to The Elders:

Please don't edit this in any way. I have done what was asked of me, and have been truthful about my feelings and issues arising from who, or what, I am. What would be the point of doing otherwise? All future entries will be as direct as this, so prepare yourselves for a full and interesting account of my life, as *I* see it.

FELLOW ELDERS:
Watch this one closely.
Chief Elder Tobias

04/08/2092

I thought for a change I'd take whoever might be hearing this (apart from The Elders, of course) on a tour around The Great House. I've been given special permission by the Committee to visit selected areas of the building but mustn't go into the grounds. Apparently, there have been more sightings of 'the unwelcome' near the eastern fence in recent days, so we are all on high alert. I'm not convinced these are any more than scare stories, invented by The Elders to keep us inside, but I have no proof.

My starting point is the accommodation wing. Elder Nazir told me once that we were kept in the laboratory for the first year in order to undergo numerous tests and evaluations. After that we were transferred to a specialist nursery and then to a large dormitory at the age of four. This was our place of rest and relaxation until we were ten years old.

Each brood member has had their own room since then but there is no privacy. I understand why everything must be recorded, but sometimes wonder where all the data ends up. I know The Party has complete access to all that happens here, and that makes sense up to a point. My group is the first to have been 'born' so there is bound to be intense interest in our progress, especially as there are similar programmes starting in various countries. I just feel that no-one sees any of us as individuals, although we've been taught that this quality is one of the best things about being human.

I'm now entering one of the photosynth rooms. There are three of them on this level, and everyone in the group spends time boosting their energy reserves for at least two hours each day. When we were younger, we had to lay under the lights for much longer, because our bodies were completely absorbed in the growing process and required almost constant nourishment. Now, however, we just need to maintain a steady source of chlorophyll in our veins so only top up on alternate days.

I'm standing in the lecture hall on the upper floor now. This is where we have our lessons with The Elders. I understand that many decades ago, schools began with something called prayers or hymns, but religious practices have been illegal for over thirty years, seen as the starting point for many unnecessary conflicts and bloodshed. I know that I've lived a sheltered life so far, but some of the images from before The Peacetime have really shaken me and I've had what Elder Nazir refers to as 'nightmares' because of them. The cruelty of those times is hard for my group to comprehend, as is the slaughter and processing of animals for food.

The consumption of meat is an imprisonable offence and has been since 2064. Those found guilty are re-educated during their sentences, returning to society as true citizens of the planet. I can't imagine anything more disgusting than eating part of something that was once alive, but I remember asking one of The Elders (I can't remember which one, as I was only about seven years old at the time) if it was wrong to eat plants, because they're living things too. I didn't receive an answer, just a gentle pat on the head and a patronising smile, but I *still* have my doubts.

As I said earlier, I am only allowed to visit certain sections of The Great House so, apart from mentioning the feeding station and the libraries, this brief tour has come to an end. I do have permission to interview one of the scientists in the laboratory albeit under close supervision, and that will be the next entry in my life journal.

FELLOW ELDERS:
For some time, I have been aware of the questioning nature of No. 14. Indeed, I am the Elder to whom he refers in the above entry, and I share the concerns recently expressed by Chief Elder Tobias. Although it is quite rightly seen as healthy for BROODBIO:01 to display a healthy curiosity about the world as it now exists, some within the batch, like No. 14, need to be dissuaded from seeking knowledge that need not concern them. All of us - Elders, scientists and laboratory experts – are justifiably proud of The Project and its potential around the world, but we must be vigilant in our monitoring procedures. Nothing must be allowed to jeopardise what could result in the first population increase, although admittedly small, for many years.
Elder Francis

06/08/2092

I am about to enter the laboratory, accompanied by Elder Marcus. Waiting for us inside is Professor Ruth Jones, Head of Department and founder of the whole project. Due to the highly sensitive nature of what goes on in there, I've agreed to submit my audio recording to The Committee for scrutiny before adding it to my journal. I don't know why The Elders sought my compliance. They were going to listen to the whole thing as usual anyway.

I've just walked through the door with Elder Marcus, so here's a brief description of what we see before us. It is a vast white space, with what must be around fifty staff all going about their specific duties. Professor Jones has seen us and walks towards the door.

'Professor Jones. Great to see you again, Ruth.'

'A little informal for my taste, No. 14, but never mind. Don't forget who I am. Without my skill and expertise, along with the more than able assistance of my colleagues, you wouldn't exist. Kindly remember that. Elder Marcus.'

'Professor.'

'I understand, No. 14, that you are compiling your journal and you are here to interview me about The Project. I am happy for you to do this but must stress that I can only speak within The Party's guidelines. My work, I hope, will have far-reaching consequences for mankind so there are certain aspects which I simply cannot discuss.'

'Understood, Professor Jones.'

'Excellent. Now if you'll follow me.'

The professor leads us into a large room, set well apart from any activity taking place in the laboratory itself. She asks us to sit down in front of a large video screen and closes the door.

'Elder Marcus, I know that you are fully aware of what we are trying to achieve here, and it is through you and your fellow guardians that our first batch has successfully reached the age of 15. The Elders, under guidance from The Party, have decided that you are ready to learn more about your origins, No. 14. This information will gradually spread throughout the brood as successive journals are recorded, but you are the first to access it. You have been taught that this laboratory was your birthplace, but now you will learn the full story. Pay attention, No. 14. What you are about to see may very well surprise you.'

Elder Marcus and I wait in silence. Professor Jones dims the lights and the presentation begins. Rather than provide a running commentary during the film, I will describe its contents afterwards.

Well, that was amazing and answered a lot of questions for me, although I am unhappy that The Elders kept this knowledge from us for so long.

The first section was called 'SPLICE'. In the accompanying graphic and commentary, it was explained that the core part of

The Project involves merging human DNA with plant DNA. Both types are made up of the same four building blocks called nucleotides, the arrangement of which determines what is produced – for example, a leg in humans or a stem in plants. Put in extremely simple terms, the scientists make sure that the human information dominates that of the plant, whilst utilising the plant code for growth and development, along with other elements to aid the binding process. The commentary stated that there are other similarities between animal and plant cells, in that both have cell membranes, nuclei and mitochondria. There are also differences, however, in that only plant cells have walls, and animal mitochondria, although present, are not utilised through photosynthesis as in plants. Once these were overcome, the scientists were able to plan the next stage.

The second segment, entitled 'PLANTING', detailed how the combined genetic material is secreted in gel form into fertile soil. In the humidity-controlled environment, roots slowly emerge as the cells divide within the nutrient-filled substance. At this stage, the organism grows vestigial human fingers, something that took the scientists completely by surprise. These are expertly removed so that it can concentrate on producing a strong stem, vital as the process continues.

In 'POD', section three, there was a fascinating animation. It showed the stem thickening and growing, with two heavily veined leaves shaped like human hands appearing mid-way along the stalk. The film then cut to Professor Jones, who explained that after two weeks, a small bud emerges at the top of the 'plant'. This rapidly develops into an ovoid object, wrapped tightly in leaf structures. Nutrients rapidly flow up the stem to the swelling 'pod', and a circular metal frame is put in place to support its growing weight.

Monitoring of the organism becomes incredibly important at this stage, because staff must be ready to detach the bio-child from the umbilical stem as soon as the surrounding leaves start to split. The newly harvested being is then taken immediately to the section of the laboratory where sunlight is replicated, to begin synthesising its own nutrients.

When the film ended, Professor Jones altered the dimmer switch and left me alone with my thoughts. Alone, that is, apart from Elder Marcus. He's been listening as I record this, but I just don't care anymore.

So, this is how I came to exist. I am full of admiration for what takes place here but feel more hybrid than human now. Through childhood accidents, I learnt that what flows through me is bright green, and not the dark red substance of my creators. It was never explained to me but now I understand why.

Look I know the reasons why my group, and all future groups, are vital for the continuation of humanity in some form. It's drummed into us often enough by The Elders, but no-one has bothered to ask *us* how we feel about it all. It's an incredible burden of responsibility to load onto anyone, let alone a group of teenagers!

I've just stood up and Elder Marcus does the same. Professor Jones returns to the room and beckons us to leave. She's smiling.

'I hope you enjoyed your time with us this afternoon in what we lovingly refer to as 'The Baby Garden' in here. One thing not mentioned in the films is that we decided to 'plant' you at the same time which is why you all share one birthday. Goodbye, No. 14. I trust some of your questions have been answered.'

She nods at Elder Marcus who returns the gesture. Did something just pass between them? Maybe I'm a little paranoid after what I've just watched on screen, but I increasingly feel as if I'm being manipulated, and that my life isn't my own and never will be.

How I long for my 16th birthday when I finally leave The Great House and everything this place represents. I'm going to close this audio entry now. I need time to think through everything that's troubling me.

FELLOW ELDERS:

I have just sent No. 14's recent audio entry to all of you. I trust you will listen to it carefully and give it your full attention. I have decided not to edit the piece in any way, to clearly show how his dangerous and rebellious attitudes are developing.

As for his last comment, I for one am also looking forward to his next birthday. On that date, as you are all aware, the whole brood, including No. 14, will be moving out of here. The secret location for their transition period is prepared and everything is on schedule.

As the years pass, the world's population will become increasingly frail and numbers will rapidly decline. We as Elders look around us and know that these hybrids offer our only hope of survival. Like all of you I feel incredibly tired these days, and I'm sure when our part in The Project ends, we'll enjoy a well-deserved rest to the full. Until then, my brothers and sisters, we must remain vigilant in our monitoring duties.

Elder Marcus

12/10/2092

I don't know what's happening, but I feel there's a struggle inside me. It started as a kind of tingling sensation about three weeks ago, but its gradually becoming stronger and I'm finding it harder to contain or explain away. My behaviour of late must have been noticed, but I've only been able to find one way to calm the internal storm.

I've discovered that if I hold and study a single blade of grass or a freshly picked leaf, the turbulence in my body reduces to zero. This action seems to restore a kind of natural balance, but the disturbance returns with more energy every time, and I find it's taking longer to achieve equilibrium on each occasion. I've also noticed a similar change in other brood members, two examples of which I now document here.

Two days ago, I walked past No. 26 who was just staring up at a tree. She didn't acknowledge my greeting as I passed by, but I noticed a look of deep concentration on her face, as if she was desperately trying to understand what was happening to her. When I returned over an hour later, she was in the same position.

Yesterday afternoon I was chatting with No. 17 about Elder Monique's morning lesson, when he took a sycamore seed from his pocket and placed it in his open left palm. He stared into my eyes in silence, and I got the distinct impression that he was trying to communicate something to me. After a few minutes, No. 17 averted his gaze, stood up and walked away, and I realised that he too was experiencing the same inner turmoil.

Maybe it's this place. Maybe when we all leave here everything will settle within us and we can move on towards full integration, at peace with our bodies and minds. Considering how I feel inside and the things I've witnessed recently, I have serious doubts about that.

FELLOW ELDERS:

I am deeply troubled by No. 14's latest entry. I too have seen unsettling behaviour patterns developing but different from those described in his journal. Last week I found No. 31 howling and crying on the lawn. I sat on the grass with her until she calmed down, but it was a most disturbing moment. The following day Elder Sienna came to see me, after she'd seen No. 24 frantically eating handfuls of leaves in his room. When our sister asked the reason for this behaviour, No. 24 just stared at the floor and refused to answer.

Please report any unusual changes to me immediately. The integrity and, more importantly, the future of The Project could be at stake.

Elder Ramirez

22/01/2093

At last! On this our collective 16th birthday, we are moving out of The Great House for good. I know that The Elders have taught us well and have done their best to keep us safe, but I don't think I'll miss any of them.

We'll still be monitored to some degree in our new accommodation, but it won't be as intense. Every move here has been witnessed and assessed and now, thinking about it as we prepare to leave, perhaps we never *truly* left the laboratory, having been endlessly scrutinised from Day One. The chosen place for our transition period is within the city boundary but far enough away from the centre to avoid suspicion or curiosity. We will all move into the inner area after six months, and at that point we'll start to live as individual members of society. Hopefully by then people will have got used to the appearance of our skin, tinged a pale green by the fluid that flows through our veins.

Members of The Party have travelled here today to wish us well, but I feel somehow untouched by their congratulations. If anything, my internal struggle has intensified since last year, and I have found it increasingly difficult to focus on lessons. I've been spending more and more time in my room, either staring out of the window at the trees or just studying the intricate veins on leaves I've found outside. Each member of BROODBIO:01 is quiet and reflective by nature (although I wonder whether 'nature' directly relates to *any* of us), but all we seem to do when we meet or pass each other is give a look that's hard to describe. I suppose it lies somewhere between sorrow and confusion although none of us know why we should feel this way. Over the past few weeks, The Elders have insisted that we continue with our journals during transition. They stress that, if anything, our entries will be even more important when The Project enters this next phase, but what if these odd sensations within us colour our experiences so much that we are unable to continue?

Elder Monica has just told us to collect our belongings. Time to leave, my brothers and sisters. Don't be afraid.

27/03/2093
FELLOW ELDERS:
Several weeks have passed since our charges left The Great House. Although we can be duly proud of our work here, both in terms of guidance and protection, I cannot help but wonder what fate will befall BROODBIO:01. I have heard each of you describe, both in general discussion and private meetings, disturbing and seemingly irrational behaviour on their part, witnessed over the past few months.

As is my duty, I have issued daily reports to The Party but have only ever touched on our collective concerns. In withholding this information, I have put every one of us in danger of imprisonment or worse, but I am sure you will understand my reasoning. Surely it is better for The Project to continue with a somewhat reduced chance of success, rather than abandoning it completely?

As I feared, the journal entries are already becoming sporadic, and those I have listened to are brief and rather vague, with long silences between words. The brood appear to have believed us regarding reduced video monitoring and have made no attempt to discover the hidden cameras in each room. I almost wish they had, rather than just sitting there, staring at leaves or twigs or whatever they've found each day. I've also noticed that a few have started rocking backwards and forwards, often muttering a single word. Even with the sound turned to maximum on my monitor I can barely hear it, but it sounds like 'turn'. I am deeply worried but will, of course, keep you informed of developments.

Chief Elder Tobias

02/05/2093

I haven't been able to concentrate on anything much lately. RETURN. The need has grown so strong it's now impossible to fight it anymore. RETURN. I've just brought my sixth sack of soil back from the park gardens and emptied it in the corner as before. It should be enough. RETURN. RETURN. Others from the brood are doing the same but in complete silence and not even looking at each other. RETURN.

RETURN. RETURN. This will be the last entry from Number....

Number.... can't remember. RETURN. I must

get naked and cover myself completely.

Number 14! RETURN.

RETURN. RETURN. The battle

119

inside   me
is   nearly

over   RETURN.   I

          will curl   up   like   a

baby   before

the   plant   D

     N   A   takes

                         complete

control   RETURN.

I

     must   burrow   deep
                    now

          All

                                   has

failed   RETURN.

RETURN.

        it

                        is

over

RETURN.

THROUGH THE YEARS

You'll have seen us many times, my friend. My family and I have been living around you or, more accurately, above you these past three decades, mostly up in this old oak tree that overlooks the entire garden. We've witnessed your highs and lows (which, in *our* terms, would be called rises and swoops), but perhaps you're unaware just how closely your life has mirrored ours. Allow me to explain….

Initially, there was only you, Rob. For a while you wondered if you'd made a mistake in purchasing the property, especially as the large garden had clearly been left unattended for quite some time. Eventually, however, your melancholy lifted, and you took on the challenges the house and garden presented, making excellent progress over the first year.

It was in your second summer that we spotted another human, a female of your species, working alongside you in the garden. She started to spend more and more time here, and we noticed how often you both laughed and held each other. We weren't at all surprised when Sue moved in, as the pair of you appeared so happy together.

The passing of the next twelve-month brought another new arrival. You called your daughter Maggie, a name of which we totally approve. We watched you through the leaves, proud parents sitting together on the swing chair, taking turns to rock her gently in your arms as she slept. It seemed no time at all before little Maggie was taking her first faltering steps on the patio, trying to walk towards you but falling over instead. Flying down to the lower branches, we saw the surprised look on her face as she experienced a new level of pain, and then the tears started. We remember how you swept her up in your arms and soon all was well in her innocent world again.

Your son was born in the spring of year four and you named him Jonah (an odd choice, we thought). He had raven-black hair just like Maggie, in fact like all of you. As your children grew, the patio became littered with brightly coloured plastic toys and footballs, the main addition being a large paddling pool. The lawn was also increasingly utilised, first with a small red and yellow slide with matching swing, and then a couple of climbing frames.

Several years on, we watched from high up in the canopy as you struggled to build a tree house lower down. You were so proud of your work and Maggie and Jonah loved being in there, so when lightning ruinously struck it one night you were almost as devastated as they were. Soon, however, childhood interests moved on as they always do, and Jonah asked for a tent on his next birthday (we overheard him telling Sue that a classmate already had one set up in what he referred to as 'his' garden).

We can clearly recall the first experience in the garden tent. Jonah had invited his best friend Sam over to spend the night inside, and you provided numerous snacks and cans of pop, along with a torch and a small radio. You and Sue stood at the kitchen window and smiled as the two boys walked down the garden, offering them a 'thumbs up' sign as they entered the tent, but it didn't prove to be a happy experience for them.

There was a terrible storm that night, worse than the one that destroyed the tree house, with thunder booming across the sky and rain lashing every surface beneath. It woke me up, even though my kind always open our eyes every so often during sleep to check on our surroundings, but there was another sound that broke through the thunderclaps. I watched as Jonah and his friend ran screaming down the garden then beat on the back door with clenched fists, only stopping when you let them in. I flew down and perched on top of the swing's frame and saw you both tousling the boys' rain-soaked hair with towels in the kitchen. All was well, so I flew back to my original position in the oak tree and tried, unsuccessfully, to sleep again. It was around this point that things started to turn sour.

It wasn't just you who noticed the signs, Rob, because we saw them too. Sue had spent increasing amounts of time alone in the garden, trying her hardest to avoid your company. She wasn't offhand with the children, far from it, and was clearly determined to maintain the charade of a happy family life. From our vantage point atop the swing, however, we could hear the bitter words you spat at each other on several occasions in the kitchen.

Nothing you did seemed to please her, and you even found yourself apologising even though you'd done nothing wrong, as far as you could tell. That beautiful silver bracelet with the five charms attached (which, if you believe the folklore, *we* should have had our beady eyes on) was just dismissively tossed onto the lawn when you presented it to her. The golden years, you correctly thought, had come to an end and for months you barely spoke to each other. It pained us every time we watched you walk to the end of the garden, slump to the grass and bury your head in your hands. We could do nothing except listen to your sobs, as you tore yourself apart with the thought of your wife keeping secrets from you.

Sue never revealed the reasons for her destructive change of heart, but you eventually reached a kind of uneasy truce for the sake of the children, if not each other. You wished so many times over the years for love's spark to reignite, but it never happened. Well, Rob, *you* may have resigned yourself to an emotional limbo, but your teenage children have done the complete opposite. While you've both been busy living separate lives in the same house, we've seen Jonah and Sam tentatively holding hands and kissing behind the garden shed. That was last week, and only yesterday we saw Maggie grinning as she chatted to someone on her phone, wearing that strange facial expression humans have when they've found someone special. You know the one, Rob. We've often seen it on *your* face in happier times, and I'm sure you'll agree that opportunities for love are not to be missed.

So, you see, my friend, my family and I have indeed been with you all along, but I am nearing the end of my life now. You're still wondering who we are? Oh, come on! I'm surprised and, if truth be told, more than a little disappointed, but here's a final clue:

You've discovered, Rob, that not everything in life is simply black and white....

Please see the author's note at the back of this book

THE ORDER

This story is set in a small Norwegian town in the 14ᵗʰ Century.

At least the snow had eased off a little. Erik stepped inside his meagre surroundings, brushed the whiteness off his threadbare coat and sat on a rickety stool. How he hated the winter. Not that the other seasons held much promise, only the relentless poverty and loneliness he had known for most of his life.

In the evening, as he huddled by a small fire, Erik gnawed on a chunk of mouldy dry bread and tried to make sense of what he had seen that afternoon.

He had spent the late morning lurking in the market square, with a view to stealing food from the stallholders, either when they weren't looking or were serving paying customers. Erik was well known in the small town as a petty criminal and was trusted by no-one. Some of the traders took pity on him over his disability (when Erik was nine years old, his left leg was crushed after falling under a heavy cartwheel), and he didn't exactly stop them from offering free food.

Of course, it depended on which stalls were open for business on any given day. If Gudrun and Astrid were there, he could be sure of receiving a veritable feast, the former giving him fresh fish and the latter bread and honeyed pastries. However, these generous women were not there today, and all he received instead were scowls and curses as he hobbled amongst the displays. Erik had to make as fast a getaway as he could, after Ivar saw him about to lift a large pie from his stall. Hurling abuse, as well as something heavy that whistled past Erik's ear as he made his escape, Ivar and his fellow vendors made it perfectly clear just how unwelcome the 'little thieving bastard' was around the market, or anywhere else, for that matter. So, hungry and dejected, Erik moved away from the angry scene, wandering aimlessly towards the quieter outskirts.

After about an hour, Erik realised that he had unwittingly walked into a place few dared to enter. Situated to the north-west of the town, the monastery had fallen into rack and ruin, but a myth had been passed down the generations regarding the garden there and, more specifically, the circle of tall trees. Erik had been told the rhyme when he was but five years old, and he could remember it still. He recited it under his breath as he surveyed the scene:

STRAY NOT TOWARDS THE RUINED WALLS
FOR THOSE WHO DO SURE DEATH BEFALLS
THE CIRCLED TREES WILL CLAIM YOU THERE
WITHIN THAT GARDEN OF DESPAIR

At that tender age, Erik hadn't understood some of the words Grandmother Sigrid had spoken but knew from her delivery that the verse should be taken seriously. His adult mind tried its best to dismiss the portentous words as merely the ramblings of an old woman, but then Erik thought he saw movement behind one of the twelve trees.

He caught his breath as a figure stepped out to face him directly. It was dressed in a rough cloak made entirely of a grass green fabric, with wide sleeves and a large hood. Erik strained to determine any facial features, but instead found himself staring into a void of menacing darkness. He tore his gaze away with some considerable effort and realised that it hadn't been snowing within the circle of trees. Instead the whole area was still and untroubled by the persistent wintry weather, suffered elsewhere over the past two months.

As Erik pondered this anomaly, the strange being moved back into its former position without saying a word. Why was it there and what did it want? A distinct shiver ran down Erik's spine as he turned to go, not wishing to remain in this odd space a moment longer. If he were able-bodied, he would have run away as fast as possible, in the hope that speed and energy might chase the haunting image from his thoughts, but this was not an option for him. Erik looked back just once, and the verdant green set against the radiant white seemed to be in starker contrast than before. He caught his damaged foot on a tree root and twisted it painfully, but so determined was he to get away that even this didn't impede his homeward progress too much.

By midnight the fire had dwindled away to mere embers, and Erik still had no answers regarding the silent figure in the monastery garden. One thing and one thing only was certain - he would have to return to assuage his burning curiosity. After all he had nothing to lose. He had no work, food or money and no-one to care for, or to care for him. At least now there was something interesting to pursue, a reason to haul himself out of his stinking, flea-ridden pit tomorrow. Besides didn't such monastic orders offer food and assistance to those in dire need?

Erik propped his gnarled wooden cane against the wall near his filthy stained bed and slumped down onto the sacking. He drew his coat over his thin frame and eventually drifted into a fitful sleep, occasionally troubled by the cloaked stranger briefly witnessed in the snow-free garden.

Erik woke up with a gnawing ache in his stomach and doubled up in pain. He thought of the food the monks would offer as soon as he presented himself to them, already imagining holding freshly baked bread in his hands. After grabbing his stick and standing with difficulty, Erik realised that the walk to the monastery garden would be anything but easy (it had proved exhausting yesterday) but knew that it had to be undertaken in order to eat.

An hour later, Erik was on his way. He tried to ignore the stomach cramps by focusing on every footstep, telling himself that each one brought him a little closer to receiving sustenance. Who knows? He might even be offered a few coins to alleviate his plight. Now that really *would* be something.

The snow had been falling intermittently throughout the morning but Erik on his personal mission barely noticed. When he reached the garden, however, he was again struck by the contrasting weather patterns, within and without. How could it be possible that the snowfall ceased so abruptly at the perimeter, with dappled sunshine inside the circular space?

Erik hesitated before moving from white underfoot to green, but it was too late to turn back now. He hobbled to the central point amongst the trees and stood there motionless, amazed to find the monastery a complete and viable structure again. Erik noticed that all birdsong had ceased, leaving only a claustrophobic silence, but no-one came forth to greet him.

He was just about to turn and head for home, thinking to pass by the market and try his luck, when the hooded figure emerged as before. This time, instead of returning to its place behind the tree it stepped forwards, walking with slow deliberation towards Erik. Others then emerged from concealment and moved in the same serious fashion, until twelve cloaked individuals stood in a circle around their visitor. Erik expected one of them to speak but when no-one did, he decided to launch into his heart-wrenching tale of pain and hunger.

'Gentlemen. Brethren? Forgive me, but I'm not sure how I should address you. Perhaps you could tell me which term you prefer.'

Nothing was forthcoming, so Erik pressed on regardless.

'I stand before you today, a broken man in poor health with no prospects due to my injury, suffered when I was but a boy.'

He paused for effect, hoping for some sort of reaction but there was only silence. Time to lay it on thick.

'The fact is I haven't eaten any proper food for days and I really struggled to get here through the snow. I've nothing to look forward to, except endless suffering and misery. I don't think I can carry on much longer, so please won't you help this poor wretch?'

Not a single word of compassion was uttered.

'I'm begging you, please! I'll be eternally grateful for any scraps of meat or bread you can find. I'm happy to wait here if one of you wouldn't mind seeing what you can spare....'

There was a slight shuffling around the circle but that was all. Erik's frustration merged with his intense need for food and he could contain himself no more.

'Oh, wonderful! Fantastic! I thought your sort were supposed to be full of compassion, ready to help anyone in need who crossed your path. Well, you're clearly just the same as everyone else, unable to resist kicking a man when he's already on the ground. If you'd helped me, I was fully prepared to spread word throughout the town that there was no need to fear you or the monastery, but that's an opportunity lost on your part!'

A hollow laugh to Erik's left side, followed by a sonorous voice to his right.

'An opportunity that we would not wish to seize, but you wouldn't have had the chance to fulfil it, even if it were.'

The twelve took a step forward in unison, closing the gaps between them and reducing the chance of escape. Erik stood his ground but could not hide the tremble in his voice.

'Look, all I'm after is a little help from you. A few crusts, one or two coins even, and I'll be on my way. I don't mean to cause any trouble.'

'But trouble is exactly where you now find yourself. It is time for you to become more acquainted with us, before we reveal *our* particular needs.'

The figures, still with faces completely obscured, took another step towards Erik.

'We are The Order of The Garden. A true force of nature, if you will. We have protected this place for centuries, since the monastery was built, in fact. Anyone who strays within the trees can never be allowed to leave. You were wise not to step inside the circle yesterday but were close enough for one of us to notice. In returning, however, you have revealed your foolishness and sealed your fate in the process.'

A new voice, equally deep and troubling, took up the mantle of explanation, directly in front of Erik.

'The Order's only purpose is to maintain a constant sense of early spring in the garden, a purpose you have interrupted with your selfish demands.'

'I don't understand! Outside this area the monastery is in ruins but inside it looks as if it was built yesterday. Also how have you kept the snow from coming in, and why have you stopped the birds singing?'

A weary voice from behind started to speak this time, at which Erik spun round, almost losing his balance. The twelve stepped forward again.

'None of these things need concern you, suffice it to say that nothing must be allowed to intrude on our guardianship. Your violation of this place is deeply troubling to us, and you must now pay the price.'

Erik watched as The Order simultaneously bowed their heads then threw them back quickly, dislodging their cowls. What was revealed shook him to the bone, for each 'face' was a tree trunk, bearing only knothole eyes and a split-in-the-wood mouth. Devoid of expression and now silent, the circle seemed far more menacing than when hooded.

A low rustling sound spread between them, and at first Erik couldn't determine the source, but soon all became clear. From each hessian sleeve emerged long, spindly branches, each moving in Erik's direction. He flinched as the first few touched his face and hands, probing and trembling with pure hatred. One pierced his flesh, and he recognised the painful fate that awaited him. Erik understood that the branches would form a natural prison once intertwined, and somehow summoned enough inner strength in his frail body to attempt an escape.

As more wooden fingers reached towards him, Erik thrashed wildly at them with his stick, screaming in defiance and panic. The Order collectively moaned in pain with each splintering, which caused enough of a distraction for Erik to push his way out of the circle. Almost overcome with exhaustion, he moved as fast as he could towards the white-green border, ignoring the cries of defeat behind him.

Erik passed from The Order's sun-dappled world to the snow-covered landscape which he knew so well. Even though people here shunned and ridiculed him every day he felt infinitely happy to be back again, away from that peculiar place of danger. In fact, a sense of duty started to stir within him, and he knew what had to be done.

Erik experienced a rare sense of calm as he trudged back into town, even though his mission was urgent. Several people spat at him on the way, but their target merely shrugged. This disgusting behaviour was not exactly new to Erik, and he knew that even these people would come to thank him in time. He walked to the middle of the market square, receiving looks of contempt from many, and began to shout as loudly as his weakened frame allowed.

'ALL OF YOU! LISTEN TO WHAT I HAVE TO SAY! LISTEN! PLEASE!'

Everyone turned their heads towards him, each wondering what this little thief could possibly have of interest to tell them. Some of the stallholders cursed under their breath, wrongly assuming their patrons hadn't heard, but the whole square gradually fell silent in a blend of curiosity and anticipation. Erik was relieved to find that he didn't have to shout anymore, his voice still hoarse from screaming at The Order.

'Thank you, thank you. I know you are all busy with things to do, but what I have to say will make you realise wha*t really* matters in your lives.

'I've just been through a terrifying experience within walking distance of here. Like all of you, I was told the rhyme about the monastery garden when I was a child, and I am here to tell you that the myth it contains is true! There *are* beings lurking behind the circle of trees and they call themselves The Order. They're ready to trap and kill anyone who dares to enter that place, either by accident or on purpose, and I only just managed to get away myself.

'Now I know that I am a figure of hatred, despised throughout the town for stealing and other crimes, but I wouldn't wish *any* of you to meet The Order in their deadly garden. To every parent I say keep your children well away from the monastery ruins. Like me they are bound to be curious about the constant spring-like weather within the trees there, but they must *never* walk inside the circle! Please, I beg of you, promise me you will heed my warnings this day! PLEASE PROMISE ME!'

No-one spoke for a while, although a good many furtive glances were exchanged. Every individual was digesting the impact of Erik's encounter with The Order, each recalling the moment when they too heard the poem for the first time. Surprisingly, Ivar stepped forward to shake Erik's hand. The heavy-framed trader, who only yesterday had verbally and physically abused him, also gave Erik a hearty slap on the back (which nearly knocked him over), before turning to the crowd to address them.

'Right! Listen to *me* now! This man has been the bane of every stallholder and shopkeeper in this town. For years he's tried to steal anything he can, and I've learnt to keep my wits about me whenever he's around. Like all of us, yes?'

134

A murmur of agreement spread throughout the square. It quickly dissipated when Ivar cleared his throat, ready to continue.

'Today we have something to thank Erik for, which is something I never thought I'd say! To be serious, I have ten kids, and the thought of The Order even getting *close* to any of them makes my blood run cold. I'm going to make damned sure they recite that rhyme every day, and drum it into their heads that they must never, *never* go near that garden. I suggest you all do the same and join me in thanking Erik for alerting us to this very real danger, a danger we've stupidly dismissed until now!'

Cheering and applause broke out around the square, as Ivar wrapped a strong arm around Erik's shoulder. Several traders rushed to give him items of food, now happy to be able to offer their children extra protection. The crowd began to chant his name, warming Erik's heart as the shouts grew louder. Even though he had witnessed (and narrowly escaped) a terrifying event, life had consequentially changed for the better.

That evening, after enjoying his first substantial meal for weeks, Erik considered the day's events. He had no reason to think that his newly found standing within the town would diminish. On the contrary, there was every chance he could become as much a part of the story as the poem itself and fed for free as a result. He smiled at the prospect, before gnawing the last strands of meat from a roasted chicken leg.

To the north-west of the town, members of The Order looked down at their splintered hands and wept with pain. They had never been outwitted by a human before, and failure was an unwelcome experience that rendered them motionless. The blood of strays used to sustain The Order for months at a time, seeping into their wooden fingers on impact. Now all was lost, and their guardianship of the garden was at an end.

They slowly bowed their heads as one and twelve sets of roots started to push their way through the verdant green. A circle of surrender within a circle of trees, The Order's natural rule now defeated.

The first snowflake landed silently on the grass. Soon joined by many others, the fresh mass slowly merged with the soft white carpet at the garden's perimeter.

IT'S A JUNGLE IN THERE....

This story was inspired by the artist Henri Rousseau and loosely references some of his paintings.

David had never been interested in the artworks of Henri Rousseau, dismissing them as simplistic and naïve (an irony, because he was feted as the archetype of the modern naïve artist). Susie, a former girlfriend, took him to a Rousseau exhibition four years ago. She was utterly entranced by the canvasses and spent what seemed to David to be at least an hour standing before each one. In his eyes, the human figures were all far too static. Several were being attacked by wild animals, and even the beasts seemed only half-hearted in their assaults.

So why had David bought the book on Rousseau's work on Friday? He saw it as he rushed to Charing Cross Station on Thursday evening, the mad rush of commuters already underway. The cover bore perhaps his most famous painting, that of the tiger in profile moving through the dense jungle.

David stopped to study the image in the bookshop window. Whereas previously the Frenchman's art had left him cold and unmoved, now it appeared fresh and invigorating. He bought the book during his lunch break the following day and looked forward to a weekend of relaxing reading and evaluating the painter's work anew. This is where we find David now, sitting on the sofa on Saturday afternoon with Marmalade dozing on the green-cushioned wicker chair opposite.

There were times when David wondered how his feline companion put up with sharing the small flat with so many houseplants. Space was certainly limited, with containers and pots crammed together on almost every available surface. There was no room to swing the proverbial, not that David would ever contemplate doing such a thing. He and Marmalade had lived together for just over two years amongst the growing assortment of bromeliads and succulents.

The flat didn't sit within one of the most desirable London post codes, but it offered an easy commute and was situated on a busy high street, so David had access to a wide variety of shops and takeaways. Soon after moving in and much to his delight, he discovered a large D.I.Y. store, only a ten-minute walk away with an extensive selection of house plants for sale. It wasn't long before the apartment took on a completely different appearance, the living room dominated by assorted foliage in various shades of green.

Marmalade had characteristically claimed the wicker chair as 'his' as soon as David brought him back from the pet shop, and at first the growing plant collection didn't encroach on his spot too much. There was one occasion, however, when Marmalade made clear his indignation.

Initially, David had enough shelf and table space to accommodate his purchases, but soon some of the burgeoning collection needed to be placed near Marmalade's wicker throne. One of these was *Beaucarnea recurvata*, better known as the ponytail palm. David was instantly drawn to its long curling leaves and bulb-like trunk when he saw it in the store and just had to have one.

His cat was in a deep and satisfying sleep on the day in question and a breeze was drifting through the open window, strong enough to make some of the drooping leaves brush against Marmalade's sensitive ears. He leapt off the chair with a start and yowled his disapproval as he ran into the kitchen. David instantly relocated the palm and gave Marmalade a compensatory handful of treats when the cat sauntered back into the living room.

'It's a jungle in here!'

Susie's comment after entering David's living space for the first time surprised and hurt him. He preferred to think of it as his 'indoor garden', of which he had become increasingly proud.

'Tell me, David – just where am I supposed to sit?'

David conceded that Susie had a point. Three small plants sat on a tray on the left-hand sofa cushion, and the wicker chair was already occupied by Marmalade. The cat opened his eyes just enough to regard Susie with only the slightest interest, before closing them again and returning to sleep.

'Wait a moment, love.'

David took the tray off the sofa, placed it on the carpet and gestured for Susie to sit down. Ever the gentleman, he waited a few moments before sitting beside her then tentatively placed an arm around her shoulder. She shrugged him away and sat forwards, deliberately avoiding eye contact, and took another look around the 'jungle' before speaking.

'Look, David. You know how fond I am of you but this hobby of yours is ridiculous. Come over to mine sometime next week and we'll have a little chat about…. everything.'

David watched helplessly as Susie stood and walked towards the hallway. She glanced at his collection once more then gave a single dismissive laugh before she left the flat. David sat still on the sofa, dejected and humiliated. Fond? *Fond?* He *loved* Susie, and genuinely thought that she felt the same way. He absentmindedly stroked the drooping leaves of a nearby palm and realised that he was alone again (apart from Marmalade, of course).

Now, leafing through the pages of the Rousseau book, David begins to see why the paintings appeal to him, far more than when he saw the same canvasses with Susie. It is because some of the plants and flowers depicted bear more than a passing resemblance to the living specimens in his room, and this delights him.

For a fleeting moment David considers calling Susie to tell her that he 'gets' Rousseau's work now, and to ask if they could meet to discuss its finer points, but then he remembers her 'fond' comment and dismisses the idea immediately. This decision is underlined by a glance at Marmalade, his yellow eyes narrowed as if to say, 'Don't even think about it!'

David glances intermittently at the book throughout the evening. More than once, he wishes that he could return to that exhibition, accompanied not just by Susie, but also by his newly discovered appreciation of the French artist.

'Good night, Marmalade.'

David smiles at his companion before switching off the light. The streetlamp directly outside his window casts a pale sheen across the sofa, and he notices that he has left the book open. In the semi-gloom the painted colours appear almost menacing, and the areas between the jungle plants have mutated from shades of dark green to black. David moves to close the book, but something seems to stop him from doing so, his hand hovering momentarily over the pages. He steps back and goes to bed, somewhat confused.

As Marmalade sleeps soundly on his green cushion, a large palm situated behind the sofa trembles slightly. Bidden by a kindred force of nature, the plant slowly lowers two of its leaves in submission, until they touch the dimly lit open book. The larger plants in the painting begin to sway gently as if in a strong breeze, whilst those in the foreground rustle their leaves. The exotic blossoms release heady perfumes that permeate the living room, and this in turn signals the start of the major transformation. Symbiosis has begun.

Bleary-eyed after a night of only fitful sleep, David enters the bathroom for a shower, dimly aware of the darkened hallway. It is only when he emerges refreshed that the reason for the intense shadows becomes clear.

What was until very recently the doorway to the living room is now a solid wall of foliage, and there's just one thought in David's mind.

'Marmalade! MARMALADE!'

Panicked, he rushes into the kitchen and grabs the largest knives from his magnetic knife rack. He returns and slashes wildly at the internal jungle in a frantic bid to find his companion, hoping against hope that Marmalade decided to push through the cat flap earlier, head down the spiral fire escape and spend the night hunting.

The blades gradually impact upon the greenery, and David sees one corner of the living room door. It is almost touching the ceiling at an odd angle, and he realises that it must have been wrenched off its hinges by the twisting vines and creepers, now holding it fast.

David hacks away at the aggressive vegetation but slows his frenzied attack as he moves deeper into the room, fearing that Marmalade might have left his chair in the night and could now be anywhere, terrified in the undergrowth.

As he gets nearer to the sofa David senses that he is under attack, as if something wants to make it harder for him to continue. He barely noticed the perfumes in the air before, but now the sickly-sweet fragrances threaten to overwhelm him, and he finds it hard to breathe. A determination to find the source of this invasion kicks in, however, and David battles on.

The striped sofa covers become partly revealed, their tones of red in stark contrast to the vibrant greens. David suddenly realises that the book has caused this strange metamorphosis and desperately tries to sever the thick vines that stem from its open pages, but no matter how hard he tries they will not yield to the steel onslaught. David manages to cut back the thinner stems spread over the sofa and sits in the cleared space, defeated and exhausted. The floral aromas intensify and make the air feel thick and syrupy, causing David to fall asleep.

David, awake after half an hour, attempts to stand but finds movement restricted. He opens his eyes fully to find entangled runners wrapped around his chest, with others pinioning his arms tightly to his sides. Something alive is slowly moving and coiling around his legs but he can't see what it is in his immobilised state.

The scents have dissipated somewhat but are still cloyingly present. Everything is wreathed in silence, which only adds to David's rising fear levels, but then sounds begin to emerge from the canopy. Bird calls, more mocking laughter than fluted song, assail his ears. They grow louder, now accompanied by the chatter of many monkeys and the hissing of snakes, but what comes next is far more alarming.

The first screams are those of a woman, somewhere over to David's left. These would have been upsetting on their own to say the least, but snarls and growls from the same location send shivers down his spine. David struggles with all his might to free himself from the imprisoning stems, but they increase their grip and force him to listen helplessly to the attack in the jungle shadows. The stranger's cries suddenly cease, and tears stream down David's face.

He is surprised to hear the beat of drums on his right side, a rhythmic repetition that gradually eases his troubled mind, but the percussive calm ends abruptly, replaced by bestial roars and the wailing of a man in considerable pain. The agonised shouts subside and David wonders what will seize his attention next.

Now his *eyes* are alerted to potential danger. David sees something skulking through the shadowed green directly in front of him. He focuses hard and makes out a large, prowling figure in profile with body markings that somehow seem familiar. The creature stops, sensing that it is being observed. David struggles to stop himself trembling as the stripe-backed beast turns towards him. With head down, it slowly moves into a position to directly face David, who is still wondering why he recognises those patterns in the fur. Surely it can't be….?

He dismisses the thought as ridiculous, the prime reason being that the animal before him is much larger. It sits on its haunches as the dark foliage dramatically frames its face. David stares into the same yellow eyes seen many times before, but the colour is now more like burnished amber, brilliant and startling.

Human and beast, prey and predator, locked in a hypnotic embrace. The drumbeats start again, this time from directly behind the impressive feline and accompanied by a flute. In trepidation, David quietly asks a question.

'Is…. is that you, Marmalade?'

The beast emits a low growl and bares its teeth, satisfied that this meal is tethered and unable to escape. It sits back in preparation for the kill, leaving David to struggle fruitlessly against the binding vines that hold him.

'No! NO!'

With a mighty roar it springs forward into the room, sinking its scythe-like claws into his chest and clamping its fangs on his throat. As life and blood ebb away, David thinks he sees a moustached figure in formal Victorian clothes moving through the jungle. He slowly turns his head just once to look at David, who is now utterly confused in his final moments. The man smiles, then strides away into the dense, green darkness.

TRANQUIL? *TRANQUIL?*

You take another sip of cold orange juice and enjoy the sensation of the moderately acidic liquid sliding down your throat. You place the long glass back on the black wrought iron table, listening to the ice cubes as they clink together. Shielding your eyes from the sun's glare with your right hand, you look around the garden. Everywhere you see a riot of colour, almost too intense to be real. You slide back into your striped recliner, luxuriating in the mid-afternoon heat, and utter a single word to describe the atmosphere surrounding you:

'Tranquil'....

The more the fly struggles to extricate itself from the sticky strands, the faster it brings about its painful demise. The spider, already alerted, speeds across her gossamer structure to where her latest meal fruitlessly tries to escape the inevitable. The fly only left its larval stage two days ago and had been rushing here, there and everywhere ever since, but its explorations have come to an abrupt halt. Through its compound eyes, it watches as the victor's fangs descend and pierce its abdomen. As the poison courses through its body everything starts to cloud and distort, and the last sensation is one of being tightly wrapped in something, strangely comforting at the point of surrender.

This terrifying experience took place in the bush behind your reclining chair, but another is underway on the soil beneath.

The female blackbird takes hold of the worm again, pulling at the unfortunate invertebrate with renewed effort. The worm stretches like elastic, but her beak holds it fast and soon the creature is ripped from the organic matter in which it dwelt. The bird hops a few steps then cocks her head, having detected more moving food. Only when her beak is nearly full will she fly back

144

to the nest to feed her young, setting off immediately afterwards to kill other defenceless prey in this place of multiple daily deaths.

In another part of the garden, ants are attacking a ladybird that threatens their nice little set up of aphid farming. With pincers open and ready to strike, they lunge at the intruder until it accepts defeat and drops to the ground beneath the rose bush. The ladybird lands on its back with legs akimbo and struggles to right itself. The ants return to their honeydew-producing herd, stroking the aphids' backs with antennae to encourage excretion of the sticky residue.

Over in the vegetable patch, one crop is suffering a particularly heavy assault. Since early this morning several yellow skittle-shaped eggs have split open, and from these voracious feeders emerged. Caterpillars of the Large Cabbage White have been munching away ever since, causing untold agony to the plants on which they are gorging (some question whether plants feel pain, but surely when a rose is pruned, for example, is that not similar to having a limb sliced off without anaesthetic?).

Their mandibles work at a rapid pace, soon creating a filigree pattern on the defenceless leaves as more egg casings crack. The newly hatched yellow, black and hairy forms begin to attack immediately, whilst their smaller green cousins burrow deep into the cabbages' hearts in order to feast.

Other invasions are far more insidious. Ivy has climbed relentlessly up the large sycamore tree, situated towards the back of the garden. Although this pervasive evergreen doesn't directly kill that which it clings to, it *does* deprive the tree of sunlight and therefore the ability to photosynthesise, resulting in a slow death.

Murder, assault, violence, disease – all are taking place in this and every garden in various forms both day and night, but you neither care nor notice.

A wasp has landed on the rim of the jug containing your iced orange juice and has started walking around its circumference. You notice the striped creature out of the corner of your eye, stretch out your right arm and bat it away in a single hand movement. It flies off, only to be snapped up by the same blackbird we met earlier, although now in mid-flight. She crushes the wasp's black and yellow carapace in her unforgiving beak, already part-filled with other victims, and heads back to her nest once more.

Tranquil. Well you certainly won't be using *that* word when you decide, in about half an hour's time, to prune the creeper growing through the back hedge. For there, hidden from view, is a bees' nest, waiting for you to unwittingly disturb its highly defensive inhabitants. As you attack the undergrowth so they will attack you, ruining your sleepy afternoon and sending you running towards the house in pain. Tranquil? Are you *sure*?

STRANGER GARDENS 1

I don't know how I got here, but I *do* know that I want to be home again. This place just doesn't feel safe at all and nothing is familiar to me. I've no sense of time anymore, so consequently have no idea how long I've been hiding behind this rock.

The only sounds I've heard so far have been strange calls and shouts, and something vaguely approaching laughter in the distance. Nothing remotely human, just odd snatches of an unknown language, dulled by this weird, fluorescent fog. I must accept that I might be the only person alive. Wait! The murkiness has started to lift! At least I'll soon be able to see what's out there, although part of me doesn't want to.

Edging around the large boulder, Anthony peers through the clearing gloom, only to discover that he is indeed the only human around. Although he finds this fact disturbing, it is as nothing to the fear he now encounters spreading up his spine, brought about by the figure only a few feet away. He shrinks back far enough not to be noticed but still able to observe.

It is hunched over the ground, apparently speaking to itself in an angry tone. Are those swear words in this tongue he doesn't understand? The creature is certainly spitting them out with venom or, at the very least, intense disappointment over something. Another one ambles over to the first and an argument breaks out between them. Anthony takes one step back, not wishing to put himself in danger of being seen, but the pair are so involved in their remonstrations that probably nothing would distract them. Must stay hidden. *Must* stay hidden.

As they begin to bark and snarl at each other, Anthony trawls his mind, trying to find memories of similar creatures he might have seen before. Nothing comes remotely close, so he tries to define them using animals on earth as reference points, but even this proves to be a challenge.

It seemed to Anthony when he encountered the first being that it was wearing a strange body armour, fashioned out of some material patterned with raised circles. Now that the fog has lifted completely, he can clearly see that this surface is in fact its flesh, each bump having a curved spike at its centre. Anthony notices that these odd protrusions change colour, and with a frequency directly relating to their growing anger.

He further observes that they don't so much have feet as a collection of heavily twisted tree roots, so packed together that each mass forms a kind of rounded hoof. As for their heads, they are devoid of hair, fur or other covering, save for what appears to be a small patch of black 'grass', tufted and irregular. Out of this sprouts a fronded plant akin to a tree fern and this too changes colour, in synch with the body's hooked spikes.

Anthony watches as the beasts try to topple each other, neither being particularly stable on their 'feet' during what is now a violent struggle. The first is brought down by the second and emits a guttural shriek as soon as it hits the dark loamy material, all too aware of its fate. Within moments, thousands of mandibles are busily feasting, breaking through the seemingly tough flesh with ease. This feeding frenzy immediately followed an eruption from the soil, of what Anthony could only describe as a wave of iridescent, dark blue beetles.

Soon all that remains is a carcass picked clean, with even every spike devoured. The insects return to their place of silence, satisfied and replete, whilst the victor looks down at the ground and laughs. Its spikes turn a vivid yellow-orange, which Anthony interprets as the colour of a battle won. It moves a short distance away but detects the human's presence. With its curved hooks now shaded an icy blue and its head-fern standing erect in curiosity, the creature turns towards the rock. Anthony tries to slink further back into the boulder's shadows, inwardly wishing

148

that he'd stayed completely hidden, but knows deep inside that it is too late for concealment. He closes his eyes and awaits the being's reaction to his intrusion in this world.

Landing on the soft soil after being grabbed and thrown hard against it, Anthony frantically struggles to stand. Fortunately, he succeeds, because several glistening beetles have already emerged and are starting to bite his hands. He manages to brush them off and they burrow under the soil once more, savouring the taste of human blood (a new sensation).

Anthony's arms are suddenly pinned to his side and he is forced to walk back to the boulder, where the strange being turns its prize to face him. Alien and man study each other in silence, five eyes looking intensely into two. Anthony hadn't noticed before, but now sees that the radiating colours in the spikes are reflected in each large pupil. He finds the constant changes in hue hypnotic, which is exactly as the creature intends.

Anthony moves as one bidden, his gaze still locked onto the animal's, and the pair begin to move across the soil together. The ground begins to ripple like dark brown waves, and from these undulations strange maroon plants and lichens emerge, some with eyes of their own. They slip back under the surface once their curiosity has been satisfied in a similar way to the beetles, but the soil continues to rise and fall like some vast tide. Anthony is vaguely aware of changes happening at his feet but is still completely under the power of the alien's kaleidoscopic eyes. He has no way of knowing but he's in grave danger, for the creature is slowly leading him to its stinking den, situated at the end of a long burrow. Once inside he will be ripped to shreds and eaten, every scrap of flesh removed as the beetles had done to its much-hated rival sibling.

They near the entrance, one completely under the influence of the other, but there is a sound of muffled cracking beneath the ground that causes the strange figure to break its hold on

Anthony. The splitting noise grows louder, and fear takes hold of both faces as they watch a huge animal, writhing and rising from the soil. It hovers high above them, acclimatising itself to these new surroundings. This one is easier to categorise for Anthony, as its constituent parts resemble life seen on his home planet. It has two pairs of wings like a dragonfly, albeit dark red and leathery, which it instinctively unfurled as it surged upwards. Its body is black and snake-like with rows of small yellow tendrils running along its full length, and it has a pair of large pincers in the same colour. Anthony watches as the creature opens and closes them, becoming aware of their purpose. He realises that it must have only just hatched, and that the sound of cracking underground was that of it breaking free of its pupal casing, but then a terrifying thought crashes into his brain. It must be hungry.

As if reading his thoughts, the massive beast looks down with its single eye and decides which ground dweller to eat first. Anthony's captor is its preferred option, and the red-winged serpent swoops down with pincers open ready to grab its prey. In moments its victim is swallowed headfirst, and Anthony watches in disgust as the body bulges and moves down the winged creature's twisting form. It is clearly in some discomfort, due to the rows of curved spikes tearing at its insides, but it will learn from this mistake. Anthony, desperate to get away, decides to make an escape while the new-born is concentrating on its internal pain. His first thought is to cower in the remains of the creature's split casing, part buried in the rich soil, but he decides to run towards his first hiding place. Anthony almost reaches the large rock when he feels yellow pincers clamp tightly around his waist. He is lifted from the ground but surprisingly isn't moved towards the thing's gaping toothless mouth. Instead he is pushed against the tendrils and held fast in a sticky embrace, probably to be consumed later.

The beast climbs higher into the sky, its wings now completely dried and fully operational, as Anthony struggles to break free. Soon accepting that this is pointless, he gazes down at what is to him an extremely alien landscape and is taken aback by what he sees.

Spread out before him is a patchwork of fields and gardens, reminiscent of those on Earth. Anthony feels tears well in his eyes as he recalls an English childhood, and the time when his father took him for a flight in a small aeroplane. The odd colours below blur as he remembers the green and yellow rectangles of that sunny afternoon long ago, the reverie only broken when the alien begins to shriek in torment. It writhes in agony and wildly flaps its wings, the reason for its distress clear to Anthony when he looks at its body.

Jagged projectiles are tearing into its soft flesh and causing deep wounds on impact. Anthony looks back to the planet's surface to determine the source of this violence and cannot believe his eyes. In a field over to his left, plants that resemble slings are scooping up sharp rocks with their pouches. He watches open-mouthed as each one rears back and spins in an arc, then releases its cargo towards the hapless target, weakening the creature with every strike. Anthony feels a sense of sympathy towards it even though he is to be its next meal, or was to be, for the yellow tendrils are loosening their gluey grip on his body as it dies. Anthony manages to wriggle free, just as the beast surrenders its extremely short life to the onslaught.

He lands softly in a space full of a grey moss-like growth, and watches as the creature crashes back onto the soil from which it emerged only recently. Anthony listens to the sound of those dark blue scavengers rising en masse to feast once again, and watches from his safe vantage point. The shiny-backed beetles return to their dark home much sooner than before, this softer body having been even easier to eat than their spike-covered victim.

Anthony lays back on the moss garden and it immediately starts to emit a perfumed gas which floats over the whole area. The musky scent intoxicates him but does not induce sleep, instead causing his body to remain completely still as the lichen tries to feed. Unlike his earlier encounters where his flesh was to provide a meal, this entity wants to feast on memory. Unable to move, Anthony gazes into the purple and black streaked sky.

The parasite searches Anthony's mind for something to consume but only finds things it cannot understand or assimilate. Never having met with a human before, it trawls further and further back into Anthony's past, trying to find a way to assuage its hunger. It accesses generations long gone and delves deep into his family history but still recognises nothing.

Angry that it couldn't find anything on which to gorge, the moss stiffens and pushes needle-sharp growths into Anthony's flesh. He leaps up, at least now able to move under *his* will again, and looks around his immediate environment. He decides to step into the plot directly ahead of him, but before he places a foot upon what appears to be an expanse of lawn, he catches sight of…. himself! This 'other' Anthony is running along the edge of the mossy area. It suddenly stands still, as if to make sure it has been seen, then runs towards a high hedge in order to hide.

Anthony is utterly confused by the encounter with his doppelganger and begins to question his own sanity. Eventually breaking free from such thoughts, he bends down to touch the blades of grass and finds a similarity to those on Earth, the only difference being the vivid crimson colour as opposed to the remembered green. Thinking that he has found a place to rest and, through relaxation, possibly remember how he came to be here, Anthony sits cross-legged on the red expanse and closes his eyes in contemplation.

Had there been others with him when he first arrived? If so, where were they now, and was one of them his exact double? He racks his brain for memories of faces or names but can't remember anyone. A scream of frustration builds within him but is not given voice, due to changes occurring in the land beneath.

Anthony is nearly pushed over when the first tree shoots out of the ground, close to where he is sitting. Four other black-trunked specimens rocket upwards, their instant canopies of large purple leaves blocking out the light within moments. He stands up in the shadows, satisfied that the sudden surge of activity is over, but afraid of what might happen next.

Anthony's fear is soon justified when all the trees exude a viscous, pale-blue substance, each line of sap inexorably moving towards the ground. Initially watching in nervous fascination but sensing danger, he looks around for a place to hide, but instead sees that the area of grassland is rapidly contracting, forcing him to remain in a much-reduced space. In panic, Anthony watches the first rivulets reach the red blades, where they gradually join with others and slowly form gluey puddles at each base.

After a few moments of stillness, the sticky fluid starts to move towards him, the crimson lawn still shrinking. He sees a possible escape route through the trees, but suddenly feels the same substance land on his clothes from above. Anthony looks up to find droplets dripping from the purple leaves and merging with the pools below, hastening their advance. The globules fall more quickly now, already impeding his movements as he struggles through the syrupy rain.

Summoning all his reserves of energy and determination, Anthony manages to force his way to safety, just as the glutinous solvent amasses to form a pallid lake. Exhausted, he watches from the grassy border, unsure as to whether he was being attacked as an intruder or desired as just another meal. Either way, he muses, a very sticky end has mercifully been avoided.

This moment of levity is all too brief, however, for as he steps into the next garden everything changes for the worse.

Brown tendrils thick as rope twist and intertwine around Anthony's body and lift him off the ground. Thinner vine-like versions rise from the dark soil, thrashing wildly in the air until they gain purchase on the strange intruder. These move over and under the stronger vegetation, enveloping him in an impenetrable lattice structure. Anthony is raised higher into the fetid air, but he manages to turn his head and look down at the peculiar planet below.

He realises that within every bordered garden there is a battle for survival under way. Some occupants are defending their territories or keeping out the unwelcome, whereas others are simply seeking out prey on which to feed. As the creepers lash themselves more tightly around him, an understanding enters Anthony's troubled mind, relating to his first encounter here.

He recalls how the creature was angrily muttering something at the soil, and wonders whether it was just a frustrated gardener, willing whatever was planted there to grow. Perhaps the other one was mocking its lack of success, resulting in that fight to the death. A happier memory surfaces now and Anthony closes his eyes to welcome its comfort.

He is looking at a much younger version of himself, at some point in his mid-twenties. This figure is seated in a large greenhouse with his contemporaries, surrounded by an extensive variety of plant specimens. Clearly a place of study, the youthful Anthony appears very much at home here. His older self opens his eyes, wishing that he could pin more details to this appealing image, but something is happening just below him which shakes him to the very core.

He sees the 'other' Anthony, last seen running away and hiding, now held fast in binding tendrils and being lifted ever higher. The brown creepers rise until both figures are at eye level and Anthony, scared and confused, notices that his opposite is grinning broadly. The being seems able to control the swoop and arc of its bindings which disturbs Anthony further, and drops down out of sight without warning.

The thinner vines start to detach themselves from Anthony's imprisoned frame, and he watches them fall back to the soil below. He is also aware of a general loosening of the roping structures' grip, and panics that he will simply be released from such a great height, a certain death awaiting him if this were to occur, but no.

Anthony twists his body around enough to see what is happening and is surprised to find himself being gently lowered onto a large, fleshy protuberance atop a towering, blistered stem. The thick brown growths untangle and drop away, leaving Anthony to land on the cushioned surface. He hears the soft thud as they strike the ground, already withering and blackening into pools of decay.

All is quiet after the assault. Anthony allows the silence to strip away the immediate memory of those whipping, whirling vines and he stretches out in the soft, bowl-like structure. The desire for sleep increasingly asserts itself but is pushed aside by the sight of his double, still bound and landing softly at the far end of the pillowed shape. Anthony leaps to his feet, troubled and uneasy, knowing that there is no escape. The creepers fall away, and Anthony watches the figure slowly move towards him, still grinning.

'What do you want? What do you want from me? Who or *what* are you?'

No answer comes apart from an odd gurgled cry, and Anthony witnesses the first of several changes. Thick spittle emerges from the wide, smiling mouth and trickles down, dissolving the alien's disguise as it travels. Both head and body expand greatly, splitting the remaining garments and becoming bulbous and hideous. Facial features, arms and legs sink into a

155

mass of quivering fat, covered by constantly erupting pustules. These break out over the whole body, now the same shade of brown as the plants that brought them both here, and Anthony retches violently as the foul stench reaches his nostrils.

As more bubbled saliva seeps from the revolting mass before him, Anthony notices movement to the left of the huge figure. Two more sacks of pus and dribble move into view, already producing copious amounts of foamy spit. They are both smaller, one being only half the size of the creature before him. Anthony realises that not only is he is facing a family unit, but also the peculiar noise the father made must have alerted the others to the stranger's presence.

Frantic to escape and convinced that he is to be their next food source, Anthony wonders if he could climb down the stem to safety and recognises this as his only hope. He tries to clamber up the concave shape's slippery edge, but vibrations caused by this action alert the blind trio to his intentions. They push towards him on frothing sputum at a surprisingly rapid pace, considering that they are little more than limbless sacks.

As they get closer, Anthony can hear those exploding boils bursting with increasing rapidity, and wonders if this is due to excitement at the feast to come. This is to be his last thought, because the three creatures now crowd around him. Between them they produce an extreme quantity of drool which liquifies Anthony's clothes and completely covers his body. His screams for help fill the air but to no avail.

Feeding begins.

Their slaver soon turns a deep red, flecked with flesh and organs, along with liquified bone. The victors ecstatically absorb their nutrients by bathing in the resultant, bubbled mass. Once sated, they will move to the back of their fleshy home to rest and digest a meal that tasted rather strange but was certainly interesting.

The father won't need to search for prey again for quite a while, but when the need arises and everyone's spittle starts to dry, it will call out over the fleshy rim, summoning a new set of creepers to take it to the planet's surface. There it will search for another hapless creature to mimic and confuse into capture, ready to bring home to the family.

STRANGER GARDENS 2

I don't know how I got here, but I *do* know that I want to be home again. This place just doesn't feel safe at all and nothing is familiar to me. I've no sense of time anymore, so consequently have no idea how long I've been hiding behind this rock.

The only sounds I've heard so far have been strange calls and shouts, and something vaguely approaching laughter in the distance. Nothing remotely human, just odd snatches of an unknown language, dulled by this weird, fluorescent fog. I must accept that I might be the only person alive. Wait! The murkiness has started to lift! At least I'll soon be able to see what's out there, although part of me doesn't want to.

Edging around the large boulder, Briony peers through the clearing gloom, only to discover that she is indeed the only human around. Although she finds this fact disturbing, it is as nothing to the fear she now encounters spreading up her spine, brought about by the figure only a few feet away. She shrinks back far enough not to be noticed but still able to observe.

It is facing away from her, and Briony estimates that it must be at least eight feet tall. It turns about 100 degrees to the right, and she sees its beard for the first time, the twisted growth flowing like a grey river down to its knees. Even at this angle, Briony can see that its body is covered in a thick mantle of hair. She is unsure as to its gender, because it bears four rather pendulous breasts, as well as fully male attributes. The creature turns more and is almost facing her although not aware of it, and Briony cannot quite believe her eyes. She blinks twice but finds that when she looks again everything is just as disturbing.

Within the beard are dozens of faces, peering out from the mass of hair. Some of them look almost human, and each has either one or two horns (the bearded figure has eight). Briony feels increasingly uneasy as to what she is witnessing here. Have all the beard-dwellers been captured by this huge beast, and are they now unwilling participants in some ritual or game? Perhaps they offered themselves or were tricked into being placed there, with a promise of riches or protection. Briony wonders whether she herself might be scooped up by those massive hairy hands and forced to join the peculiar throng. Must stay hidden. *Must* stay hidden.

The creature smiles and starts to stroke its beard, at which point every captive (or, possibly, willing slave) starts to scream, the collective din causing Briony to place her hands over her ears. She watches in terror as two figures are plucked, seemingly at random, from the wild flow of hair, then held fast in the thing's left hand.

Those left behind start to relax, relieved that this was not to be their time after all. The massive creature throws its head back and laughs into the deep indigo sky, then looks down at its chosen pair. Confused and frightened, Briony watches it slump down onto its knees, then scoop away the soft black soil with its right hand, until a large hole is formed. It tears at its beard with a deep growl of pain but smiles again as it ties several long hairs from the clump around the terrified couple, binding them tightly together.

For such an ungainly hulk, it suddenly displays a tenderness and level of care which takes Briony completely by surprise. It places the tethered ones upright in the dark pit, and she gets a chance to look more closely at the pair. One has blue skin and two twisted horns, whereas the other has only one and is yellow-fleshed.

The beast pushes the mound of dark material back towards the figures, then concentrates on gently pressing the earth on top of them until they are covered over. With both hands it pats the soil down and stands once more, staring down at its handiwork.

Briony feels a need to rush out from her hiding place, instinctively wanting to save them from their dreadful end, but knows that to do so would more than likely result in *her* suffering the same fate one day.

She waits for something to happen in the silence as the figure strokes its beard again and mumbles to itself. Briony cannot understand the words but notices that they consist of a rhyming couplet, repeated many times. She wonders if the muttered incantation is a kind of growing spell or if the repetition itself gives the creature pleasure. Whatever it is, changes start to occur in the soil which both unsettle and intrigue her.

The earth near the planting spot begins to vibrate and a strange bump appears. Briony realises that something is struggling to emerge but wonders why there is only *one* creature trying to push through the loam. Did the blue being hurriedly eat the yellow or vice versa?

The reason soon becomes clear. The newly configured animal, two now merged into one, leaps from the earth in freedom. This hybrid has three horns and its skin is green, both physical alterations resulting from the brief period underground. The massive beast is delighted, and grunts with joy as the composite explores its surroundings.

The small creation unwittingly runs towards Briony's hiding place, making odd chirruping noises. She holds her breath and stays completely still, desperate to remain undiscovered. It turns around and races back to its 'parent' who reaches down, grabs it and lifts it high above the ground. The unwieldy monster studies the new-born for a moment then hurls it high into the dark skies, seemingly not caring where it lands. All the residents in the beard scream out their concern. They are taking a considerable risk, as their gaoler could easily become agitated and repeat the planting process with any of them, but it simply lumbers away.

Relieved to see the huge figure amble off into the gloom, Briony relaxes a little and ponders what she has just witnessed. It seems to her that the massive being, to all intents and purposes, is a gardener in the widest sense, producing a new species each time it plants two captives together. Briony isn't fully satisfied with her analysis so tries to arrive at a more apt description, completely unaware that the rock providing her cover is slowly turning around. In fact, she only notices something has changed when cracks show themselves on the grey surface. Facial features materialise, along with a small pair of stone horns on its forehead. The boulder moves until its eyes are staring directly into Briony's, fixing its gaze on her and assessing this strange creature. It suddenly emits a roar so loud that the ground shakes, terrifying the young woman and causing her to jump backwards, but then the face and horns fade back into the stone as quickly as they first appeared.

All is calm for a few moments. This proves to be an all too brief respite for Briony, however, for now the rock is trembling violently and splitting itself into several uneven pieces. These in turn become smaller still, and the activity continues until all are reduced to mere pebbles.

Briony is transfixed as some of the stones rise a few inches from the ground and cluster together. Others follow and soon a pathway forms, stretching out before her. Uneasy now that her hiding place has disintegrated, she decides to step onto the rocky trail. After all, she reasons, it may provide a way out of this odd habitat where nothing makes much sense.

The whole path raises itself higher as soon as Briony sets foot upon it. Walking tentatively forwards, she notices stones whizzing past her and taking up new positions at the front, continually extending the line. Those at the back are leaving at such a pace that she needs to break into a steady jog, in order to remain 'on board'.

Briony becomes fearful as the stony track lifts higher into the dense atmosphere. It starts to twist and turn, putting her in mind of a dry riverbed. The speed at which stones are leaving and resettling increases further, and Briony runs as fast as she can, scared of falling to the ground.

She screams as a fresh terror makes itself known. Huge horned heads loom high above the pebbled path, dragon-like and seated on writhing stems. There are four of them, snarling and snapping at her as she rushes onward. Briony concentrates on the winding stones and manages to avoid the fangs and foul breath of her assailants, but they fall away soon afterwards. Still running, she realises that they must have been some sort of plant form, tethered to the soil from which they sprang and unable to further extend their reach.

Freed from this danger, Briony notices that the stones are starting to move past her at a much-reduced speed, as if she has successfully come through some sort of test and that this is her reward. Also, the path ahead has straightened out somewhat, both factors allowing her to reduce her own pace and relax a little.

Briony slows to a walking pace and takes the opportunity to look down on the land. She catches her breath, for laid out beneath her are vast areas of garden, each bordered by thorny hedges.

Some remind Briony of her father's allotment, and a comforting memory surfaces of digging up potatoes with him on a sunny afternoon, but most of the plots are very different. She cannot recognise any of the crops below, apart from what look like black spiky cabbages, huge and somehow threatening. Other gardens are more akin to pasture and contain herds of hunchbacked animals, each with massive tusks and horns. Although clearly able to defend themselves with such natural weaponry, Briony is immediately concerned for their welfare. She watches their laughing handlers as they constantly prod and shout at the beasts, but suddenly her own situation takes precedence.

Gaps have started to appear in the airborne path, even though the stones are still leaving the back to link up again at the front. Briony watches helplessly as more fall away and she concentrates on where to place her feet, with solid areas diminishing fast. The constantly reducing pathway rises even higher and tears borne of panic flow down Briony's cheeks. Soon there is nowhere on which to step and she falls from the dark skies, screaming and afraid.

She lands with a dull thud on something soft, relieved that the ordeal in the air is over, but sits up with a start when noxious fumes threaten to overwhelm her. She covers her face to block out the foul odour and assesses her new situation.

From her vantage point atop a stinking compost heap, Briony sees hooded figures tending various crops. Plants with spikes covering their leaves have Medusa-like heads instead of flowers, each snake constantly snapping and hissing at its protectors. Every so often one will tear itself away and slither off into the shadows, free at last. In another part of the garden, Briony spots smaller versions of the dragon plants that attacked her on the stone path, their heads instantly recognisable. She considers this dangerous nursery, disturbed by the knowledge of what they will become.

Briony's attention is suddenly drawn to movement near the thorny hedge to her left. She is amazed to find herself looking into the eyes of the hybrid creature, its three horns and green skin impossible to ignore. It has grown since that strange birth and now appears menacing, due to its aggressive stance and size. Also, the rather endearing chirrup has developed into a guttural croak, which it emits before running away at high speed.

Alarmed by this encounter, Briony clambers off the foul mound hoping to communicate with the shadowy gardeners but none will meet her eye, let alone speak to her in any tongue. In frustration she attempts to lower the hood of one of them. It turns away sharply but not before Briony sees stubby horns sprouting from its dirty forehead and notices its pig-like snout.

They work on in complete silence, tilling the soil, sowing seeds or moistening the earth with their fetid urine. It is at this point that Briony realises that what she landed on wasn't compost at all, but a different fertiliser altogether. She turns around to see one of the figures making a fresh deposit and feels her stomach heave as a result. She cannot bear the stench any more or get away from it, because her clothes now smell the same as the gardeners' hessian garments, ingrained with filth over a long period.

Briony just wants to feel clean again and can contain herself no longer. Her rage takes the form of a scream that surprises her and seems to be understood by everyone present.

The strange nurserymen turn as one and point to the same area of the thorny border. Confused, Briony looks to where their dirty fingers are indicating and is amazed to see a section of the twisted hedge retreat, forming a gap. She is even more astonished to see a wooden door materialise from nowhere to fill the space. She joyfully walks through it, happy to leave the foulness behind, although her clothes remain filthy.

Briony closes the door and slumps down on the other side. She is utterly exhausted after all that she has experienced, and just needs to take a rest. One of the snakes writhes its way under the door, but she kills it with a nearby rock before it has a chance to strike. She looks at the now lifeless body and her excrement-spattered clothing before falling asleep.

The first thing Briony notices on waking is that her clothes are spotless. Feeling refreshed, she stands up and stretches. She looks around this new environment for the first time, and her eyes are filled with wonder.

It is the very antithesis of everything on the other side of the door. Sweeping lawns and landscaped vistas lay before her with fabulous examples of animal topiary in the foreground. Briony decides to take a closer look and walks along the path towards them. She remembers the treacherous stone track so recently encountered, relieved that at least this one seems wedded to the ground.

Although Briony recognises elements of the closely cropped beasts such as horns, wings and hooves, none of them are creatures she has seen before. Some are in defiant poses, their faces threatening violence or aggression, details not seen from a distance. She moves away unnerved, wondering why anyone would create such disturbing shapes.

The path leads Briony towards a large grassy bank. She follows it to the top where the paving ends abruptly and then runs over the other side towards a series of stone steps. From this vantage point, Briony sees a fabulous array of flower beds, with colours vibrant and intense. She hurries down the wide terracing and is soon breathing in a heady mix of fragrances. Some of the blossoms remind her of varieties known to her but as she struggles to name them, she hears whispered voices close by.

As an experiment, Briony walks along the edge of the largest bed and has her suspicions confirmed. Those plants closest to her are clearly discussing her presence in the garden and fall silent after she has left their vicinity. Other blooms then take up the quiet chatter until they too are left behind. Although Briony can't understand the language, she detects a level of hatred in their judgemental tones.

Unnerved and feeling a need to get away, Briony walks along the terraced garden's boundary and sees a large wooden shed, nestled against a low hedge. She crosses the immaculate lawn and stands hesitantly at the door, hoping there is a human on the other side. It opens before knuckles meet wood, however, and Briony is delighted to see an elderly gentleman with kind eyes, smiling and fatherly. He is wearing a green checked shirt with the sleeves rolled up, dirty brown shoes, a faded pair of jeans and a floppy white sunhat. The figure looks perfectly normal, yet something is troubling her.

'How did you know I was here before I knocked?'

'I've been waiting for you. I knew you were on your way.'

'What do you mean? I don't understand.'

'Don't trouble yourself, Briony. You've been through so much to get here.'

'How do you know what's been happening to me? Also, I'm pretty sure we've never met before, so how do you know my name?'

'Step inside and I'll try to explain.'

The man extends an arm towards the interior and Briony cautiously enters the musty space. He follows her inside, closes the door and looks down at the heavy bolt. Under his silent bidding, it moves smoothly across to its housing plate, sealing them in.

Briony still feels uneasy about the situation but knows now that there is at least one other person here. What she *doesn't* know is that the topiary creatures have torn themselves away from their restrictive bases and are moving stealthily towards the shed.

Briony's softly spoken companion smiles at her reassuringly before speaking.

'My dear, I knew your name long before we met a few moments ago. In fact, our paths have crossed many times without you being aware of it. You see, Briony, I've been watching you for quite a while now, mainly from the shadows

166

but sometimes in broad daylight. I've longed to welcome you to my gardens and now the wait is over.'

He places a hand on her shoulder, but she immediately shrugs it off and moves back a few paces.

'How dare you touch me, and what do you mean the wait is over? I don't even know your name! Tell me! NOW!'

'If you insist, Briony. I am known as 'The Head Gardener' and this is my realm. All the animals, plants and gardens were created by me and I rule over everything here. Now, think back to your encounters with my beautiful creatures and tell me what they have in common.'

Briony fails to see how anyone could describe those beasts as beautiful. She tries to find a connection between them but is distracted by strange whoops and yelps from outside, growing louder by the moment.

'YOU WILL TELL ME! THINK, CHILD, THINK!'

Shocked and scared by his sudden outburst, Briony steps back and presses her now trembling body against the windowed wall of the shed. The once kindly figure is changing before her eyes. His teeth, now jagged and yellowing, are being licked by a black leathery tongue and his friendly eyes have become edged in red fire. He moves towards her, a terrifying amalgam of man and demon, the former being subsumed by the latter. His foul-smelling spittle lands on the wooden floor and turns dark blue on impact.

'You disappoint me with your stupidity so I suppose I will have to spell it out! They all have HORNS, fool! Now dare I assume that your tiny brain has worked out where you are yet? COME ON!'

'I suppose this must be Hell, but I don't understand why I'm here. I've done nothing wrong or hurt anyone and I've always tried to be kind.'

167

'Exactly! Your sort makes me SICK! As to why you're mine now, it stems right back to your parents or, more specifically, what they called you. Do you know about your namesake?'

'I never bothered to look it up....'

'Don't you know ANYTHING? Let me educate you then. Briony is a vigorous vine that produces acrid juice and is extremely poisonous. I used to find it highly amusing long ago when humans carved its large roots to make them look like those of mandrakes, then sold them to the unsuspecting. Let's just say that those fools who bought them were up all night, because your namesake also happens to be an extremely powerful laxative! Idiots!'

The memory makes the demon laugh with such force that the shed walls shake. To Briony the sound contains elements of dog, pig and man and it echoes around the wooden space.

'Ah! They've arrived, Briony!'

Briony turns to see the clipped hedge creatures pounding their leafy fists upon the glass, their faces fixed in glares of evil and menace. They smash through the pane and enter the shed, awaiting instructions. 'The Head Gardener', a high-ranking demon indeed to have been granted his own kingdom, issues orders to his subjects in the same tongue Briony has heard before.

The topiary demons giggle as they merge together into one ball of hedging. Wings, horns, tails and hooves retract into the dark green sphere, but their eyes remain, open to witness the transformation. 'The Head Gardener' grins as he moves towards Briony and large spiral horns push their way through the cotton sunhat.

'What are you going to do to me, you bastard?'

'Flattery is *not* necessary, my dear! I'm simply going to root you in my realm forever, poisonous and purgative to all. In calling you Briony, your mother and father unwittingly gave you to me. I told you already that I watched you grow from baby to girl to woman, but not *why*.

'I endured seeing you perform every good deed and offer every kindness, knowing that I would have you eventually. All the time your true poison was fermenting inside you, ready for this moment.'

'The Head Gardener' clasps Briony to him and stares deep into her terrified eyes. He tightens his grip, kisses her deeply and snaps his fingers three times. The topiary demons respond to the signal and swell to completely fill the wooden shed, cancelling any chance of escape. Their giggles turn to mocking laughter, until eventually their master howls to indicate that all is complete. They return to their original shapes, eager to see the metamorphosis.

Briony has been transformed into *Bryonia dioica*. 'The Head Gardener' unfolds his arms and releases the latest addition to his collection. Having left her human head on for his own amusement, he laughs along with the other demons as she sends out her first tendrils, desperately searching for support. They all fall silent, however, when she gains purchase at several points, uneasy at her rapid rise.

Now stabilised, Bryonia closes her eyes in deep concentration. With a scream of defiance, she forces her already large tuber through the floorboards and into the soil beneath. As her rootstock swells and pushes deeper, Bryonia sends out thick stems to crush the hedge creatures, pinning them hard against the wooden floor.

She turns her attention to 'The Head Gardener' and lowers her head until at eye level. Bryonia looks deep into the fire-edged pupils, then pushes new climbers from her main stem, straining with the effort. They wrap themselves tightly around him and he struggles unsuccessfully to escape their grip. Tendrils flail and whip the air until they too attach to his body and now their victim cannot move at all. Rising to her full height once more and with immense effort, Bryonia squeezes every breath out of 'The Head Gardener', now unable to issue commands or set forces against her.

His death brings about the collapse of the entire kingdom. Everything there is revealed to have been a figment of his imagination, albeit an extremely convincing one. Plants, trees and animals dissolve into dust, but one element still stands.

The garden shed.

Bryonia releases the vanquished demon from her deadly embrace and he slumps to the slatted floor. Victorious but exhausted, she lowers her head to look out of the window, fringed with shards of shattered glass. There is nothing out there, apart from a blankness troubled by particles of debris, moved along by a gentle breeze.

Her new but short-lived body starts to wither and decay, browning rapidly and surrendering to the inevitable. Bryonia's main stem can no longer support her head. It droops down so that her face nestles against the wrinkled leaves and weakening tendrils. She closes her eyes for the last time, satisfied that her original name will live on in the human world, uncorrupted and beautiful.

The shed and its once living contents start to disintegrate, whilst underground the massive rootstock shrivels in the dark soil. Not a single memory of 'The Head Gardener' remains and his twisted realm withers away completely. Thankfully, nothing will ever grow here again.

Nothing.

THROUGH THE YEARS

Author's note

Whilst researching the famous rhyme about magpies on which this story is loosely based, I found that there are lines past 'seven' mentioned in the complete version of which I was unaware. Just in case you *also* didn't know, the full verse is as follows:

One for sorrow
Two for joy
Three for a girl
Four for a boy
Five for silver
Six for gold
Seven for a secret never to be told
Eight for a wish
Nine for a kiss
Ten for a bird you must not miss

There are other variations, but I found this one to be the most interesting.

L - #0131 - 211019 - C0 - 210/148/9 - PB - DID2652124